I0526576

The Cave of the Blue Bear

First Edition

Published by The Nazca Plains Corporation
Las Vegas, Nevada
2009

ISBN: 978-1-935509-37-0

Published by

The Nazca Plains Corporation ®
4640 Paradise Rd, Suite 141
Las Vegas NV 89109-8000

PUBLISHER'S NOTE
The Cave of the Blue Bear is a work of fiction created wholly by
Bob Archman's imagination. All characters are fictional and any
resemblance to any persons living or deceased is purely by accident.
No portion of this book reflects any real person or events.

Male Photo, Andrey Vishnyakov
Cavern, Franck Camhi
Art Director, Blake Stephens

The Cave of the Blue Bear

First Edition

Bob Archman

CONTENTS

CHAPTER 1

- Berlin 1927 -

1927 wasn't the best year to spend studying in Germany, but it was a good year for me. I was a native of the border region of France and Switzerland and I was naturally bi-lingual. My father spoke French and mother German. We were Protestant, which is unusual in France, but we were also 100% French. My father served in the Great War, but he was a pharmacist, and worked in the hospitals. He never saw active combat duty, but he knew the horrors of war first hand.

My oldest brother became a pharmacist too, but my interest was in archeology. My parents were educated and shared the interest. They approved of me becoming an academic and dreamed that I might become a Professor. No profession ranked higher in their esteem.

My parent's best friends were Dr. and Mme Dreyfus. The doctor was a brilliant and talented man. My father thought he was practicing medicine in a small city like Mont sur Le Rhone, because he was Jewish. My father was a good Calvinist and thought that anything that brought such a gifted man to our town was a blessing. "Even stupidity can bring a blessing!" he would say. The Protestant community in the city was small and we also felt like outsiders, so I think this explained my father's friendship with the Jewish family. Although no one ever said anything to our faces, we knew that we were barely tolerated.

In 1927 I had an opportunity to study under the leading professor in the subject of Neolithic Culture in Europe. Professor Erik Von Schmidt was the leading star of the University of Berlin and one of my student essays caught his attention. That is how I became a French student in Berlin.

Berlin was a very exciting place in the 1920s. It seemed as if 90% of the people were engaged in some sort of experimental project in the arts, sciences or politics. France was unpopular throughout Germany but most people thought I was Swiss and I had no problems. Berlin seemed crazy but harmless. It was lots of fun for a student in his middle twenties. Professor Von Schmidt was everything I hoped he would be. He was demanding, knowledgeable and helpful. Von Schmidt wanted the best for his students and once he realized you were willing to work, he was a friendly and outgoing man. The entire experience was wonderful.

The first person I met at the University was a spectacularly intimidating assistant to the Professor, Wolfgang Von Hellenburg. He was fearsome looking. Born Baron Von Hellenburg, he was 6'3", 200 pounds and had a blond crew cut. Wolfie turned out to be as unlike his Prussian warrior appearance as a person could be. He was very smart, clever and affable and had a wonderful since of humor.

After an hour of conversation we were friends. Stone Age archeology was his interest as well as mine and we were together much of the time. The Professor was demanding and the work was non-stop.

Wolfie's strengths were in the field, excavating. My strengths were more academic, analyzing and understanding. Together we were an unbeatable team.

He was the black sheep of his family. The Von Hellenburg's were military and authoritarian in their preferences. I met his father and brother once and was shocked at their attitudes and ideas. They were wealthy but had no taste or culture, and they obviously despised Wolfgang. Wolfie had his own money, left to him by an aunt, so he just avoided his family.

He lived in a small, but elegant apartment in Berlin, but his true love was a summer house about 100 kilometers from Berlin on the way to Dresden. He asked me out to visit him in late August. There was a break in our studies and I decided to visit him. I took a train to the nearest community and a friend of his, Max, picked me up at the station.

We drove down a country road, past a gate and through some woods until we arrived at a handsome farm house. It was old, and well restored. The house was empty but we could hear some men talking in the rear and the splashing of water. There was a swimming pool. This seemed like an extraordinary luxury to me. I loved to swim and I knew that persons of great wealth had pools but had never been anywhere with a pool.

Max and I went to the rear yard, and looked out the window and saw Wolfie, Professor Von Schmidt and two other men gathered around the pool. All were naked. I was shocked.

"Wolfgang!" Max cried. "Jean is here!" Wolfie came over to us.

So glad you could make it!" he said. I'm afraid he noticed that I was uncomfortable. "Jean, I forgot to tell you. I am a nudist in the country!" He laughed.

He was bronzed tan and muscular with covering of blond hair all over his body. At first I thought it was fine hair, but I realized it was a thick coat of hair, disguised by its light color.

"Don't worry!" he said. "You don't need to join us in our sun worship, but we are all men here so, you don't need to feel uncomfortable. Your bedroom is up stairs; Max will show you the way. It's hot, come and join us for a swim." Max took me to my bedroom. I didn't like the idea of standing around naked, but I was accustomed to nude swimming in the lakes near my home, and Professor Schmidt was downstairs, naked in the sun. I also knew that nudism was very popular in Germany and was regarded by many as having health benefits.

I was afraid that by being dressed the Professor might think me standoffish, backwards, or overly prudish. I took off my clothes and wrapped myself in a towel and went to the pool. I jumped in the pool as fast as I could and swam. I was a good swimmer and the Professor seemed to admire my technique. Everyone there seemed relaxed and by the time I got out of the water, I felt more comfortable.

"Jean," Wolfie said, "I would like to you meet Herr Professor Altenburg, he is a physician and psychiatrist." Von Schmidt and Altenburg were both big men, but Von Schmidt had pitch black hair and Altenburg was white. Von Schmidt had a mustache, Altenburg a full beard. They were barrel chested and hairy men. "And this is Max, one of my old friends from home." He had picked me up, but I didn't know his relationship to Wolfie. Max was short and with a close cut brown beard. He must have been the hairiest man I had ever seen. He was almost suitable for a carnival side show.

"And let me introduce you to Samuel Wertheimer, one of my former students," Von Schmidt said. "He is English in spite of his name." Wertheimer was rather dapper, carefully groomed and neat even when he was naked. He was quite muscular and had a hairy chest that looked as if it had been clipped.

I was trying not to look at the men's genitals, but everyone was uncut except for Wertheimer and me. Max very clearly was looking me over. I had always thought of my cock as being average in size. It was similar to my brother's and father's. They were the only naked men I was familiar with because of our swimming lessons. My father was terrified of downing and insisted that we learn how to swim.

My cock was nothing to be ashamed of in this group. Both Von Schmidt and Altenburg seem to have small members sitting on huge ball sacks. Max's cock was all but hidden by his hair. Wertheimer had a long thin cock with a big mushroom head. Wolfie's cock was bigger and thicker looking. His was almost beautiful, with the head resting deep inside the foreskin, all framed by golden hair.

I almost jolted out of my thoughts when I realized I was thinking about a beautiful cock. I had never thought of a cock as beautiful before. It was useful and enjoyable, but not beautiful.

The conversation was about German history and I soon joined in with my French outlook. Wertheimer added the English viewpoint. He spoke good German but with pronounced English accent. We were a cosmopolitan group, and everyone seemed interested in the others' views. This was unusual in Europe at this time and seemed refreshing to me. Soon I forgot we were nude. Max went in the house to prepare lunch. About ten minutes later he called for someone to help him set up the table. My parents had very firm ideas about helping the host at a party so I went to help.

It was cool inside the house compared to the full sun around the pool. Max had sandwiches ready. He wanted me to arrange them on a plate while he finished a salad.

I dropped a fork and it bounced under the table. Max got down on the floor to find it. He found the fork and my cock. All of a sudden, my cock was in his mouth, being licked and sucked. I was shocked, and didn't move. I was going to object, but it felt wonderful. It was a new but very enjoyable experience for me. Wolfie came in the room and stood beside me. Max stopped sucking me and took Wolfie's cock.

"Max!" Wolfie said. "Take care of our guest!" Max returned to my cock. "I'm sorry Jean. Max forgets to take care of our guests some times. Max and I are childhood friends, and playmates. Old habits die hard." I wanted to say something but was too confused to think what to say. I would have been embarrassed if it hadn't felt so good.

Wolfgang must have sensed this and he told Max to finish lunch. This Max did. I was almost fully erect by this time and really embarrassed to be erect in front of my friend.

"Damn it Jean!" Wolfie said, "If I had any idea you were this well hung I would have asked you here earlier! That's spectacular." The professors and Samuel entered the room and no one seemed to mind my erect cock. Everyone got a plate, filled it with sandwiches and the salad and sat down. It was as if there was nothing unusual about a naked man with an erection serving lunch.

The conversation turned to the origins of European ethnic groups. Samuel asked about Aryan origins. Von Schmidt was brutal in his analysis. "Theories are purely crack pot rantings without evidence," the distinguished professor said. "The evidence may be physical, or it may be circumstantial, but there must be evidence. There is no Aryan homeland, until someone finds it. No one has found it and no one has any evidence it exists!"

"No homeland for the master race?" Max asked.

"There is no master race," Altenburg stated firmly. "There is nothing to indicate that physical strength is associated with genius, and if Goethe is great, so are Moliere and Shakespeare." The conversation became heated. We were drinking beer and this added to the openness of the conversation.

Berlin was a center for homosexual activity at this time and I had seen transvestites and the men the English call "Nancy boys" prancing on the streets. I had no sexual experience at all. My family was very reserved and didn't want me to marry until my education was finished. My parents weren't wealthy enough to give me an inheritance, so I wasn't considered a catch to the women of my town, or Berlin for that matter. I wasn't particularly interested in women, but I had no interest in effeminate men at all.

Obviously Wolfie and Max were homosexual. I guessed that the Professors and Samuel were too. They weren't like the stereotypes of "Nancy boys" at all. They weren't like the Oscar Wilde images I held. They seemed like normal men and I liked them. I was confused and a bit excited. The excitement did nothing to reduce my erection. I wasn't fully erect, but my cock was at half staff. No one seemed to care. I wondered if erect cocks were characteristic of nudist events. Perhaps my display was of no significance.

I was tall and thin with a beard and ungainly features. Swimming gave be a muscular chest, arms and legs. They were hairy. The rest of me was smooth, except for a path of hair that connected the mat of hair on my chest to my pubic bush. I thought of myself as being patchy, completely unlike the elegance of classical statuary or the smooth bodies of movie stars.

Around three Wolfie announced that it was time for a siesta. We were to rest then return for a late dinner. I went to my room and found I was sharing it with Professor Altenburg. I was somewhat relieved that it wasn't Max. That would have been too exciting.

"I hope you don't mind sharing a room with an old man like me?" Altenburg said.

"Not at all," I replied. "It is an honor to be with such a distinguished companion." We shared the bed, as is typical in a farmhouse. My cock had almost returned to its soft state and I was relieved. Altenburg looked at my cock.

"You have relaxed," he said. "You added some excitement to our dry academic conversation." I blushed.

"I was afraid I embarrassed myself." I said.

"Not at all," he said. "The cock is the very symbol of manhood. A secret symbol, so respected that it is always hidden, except in the most primitive societies. The large cock is always respected and admired. Horse hung, donkey dicked, these obscene expressions are tributes, not insults. You were the center of unspoken admiration and desire."

"You were looking?"

"Every chance I got," he said. "As was everyone else." I must have looked uncertain. "You are a shy man?" he continued. "We are a friendly group of men. All of us are old friends. We enjoy each other's company, both intellectually and physically." I was getting hard again. Altenburg was watching my cock rise. "I know you will enjoy us as intellectual companions," he continued.

"You are a congenial group." I said, "but..." Altenburg was smiling.

"Don't say any more," he said. "I am a psychiatrist. You were erect because unconsciously you wanted your massive cock to be seen and admired. You know that it inspires those who see it. You are enjoying the admiration you can sense. If you can relax, you will find a lot more to enjoy." I didn't say anything.

My cock was hard as a rock, bloated to the bursting point. I might be unsure about Altenburg's ideas, but I realized that my cock was absolutely positive about them. Altenburg began licking my cock. My dong vanished into the mouth in the middle of his white beard.

Max had sucked me two hours earlier for the first time. I felt incredibly relieved when Altenburg began. I think I was afraid that it might never happen again. That the wonderful sensation I felt when Max sucked me would never be repeated. Max had been very vigorous. The professor was caressing my cock with his tongue and throat. It was totally different but just as exciting and pleasurable.

He pulled off. "You like it?" he asked.

"I sure do."

"Would you like to rejoin the others?" Altenburg asked. "They are at the pool, waiting for us." We got up and went down stairs. When we reached the pool I wasn't the only one there with an erection. Von Schmidt was sucking Wolfie and Samuel's face was buried in Max's crotch. I was shocked at the openness of the sex. I almost turned away, but Altenburg touched my cock. I had oozed a glob of pre cum and he spread it over my head. I shuddered in pleasure as the slippery fluid spread over my ultra sensitive organ. I realized that I had never been so sexually excited before. I was almost shivering.

"Herr Professor!" Wolfie cried. "You have converted our French friend into a member of the club?"

"I think we'd have to say he is a provisional member!" Altenburg said.

"Jean, we're glad to have you as a part of our happy band!" Wolfie said. "All for one and one for all!" He got up and came over to me. He was fully erect and impressive. His bloated cock stuck straight out and precum dripped from it. It was a bit shorter than mine, but thicker. He embraced me then sank to his knees and sucked my cock. In the next few minutes everyone around the pool sucked me.

The last to nurse on my meat was Professor Von Schmidt. When he got up he said, "Well my young student, you aren't a provisional member anymore!" He burst out laughing.

"Is this the initiation ceremony, Herr Professor?"Samuel asked. He was also laughing.

"If it isn't, it should be!" he said. "Damn, it's hot here!" He dove into the pool and we all followed. The cool water was refreshing. I appreciated the break in the sexual action. The last hour was full of new experiences for me. Nothing even faintly resembling this had ever happened to me. Quite frankly, I had never visualized anything even close to the group sexual experience of which I was the focus.

Up to this time, my idea of enjoyment was a good glass of wine and a good book. Five men had sucked my cock. Each one was both eager to suck me and good at it. I enjoyed all, but I felt the way a peasant might feel if he spent his life riding a donkey and suddenly found himself in an airplane. It was as if not only had I not been on a plane, I hadn't known such a thing existed.

My life had changed.

CHAPTER 2

- A house in the Country 1927 -

Wolfgang had christened his country house Wotan's Seat. The sign on the toilet room door labeled it the throne of the gods. He had painted an elaborate mural over the toilet of Wotan and the other members of the Nordic pantheon sitting in a ring. It took you several seconds to realize they were all on toilet seats.

Wolfie looked like a Nordic God and he had the mannerisms of a Teutonic Hero. He loved sports, opera, art, dance and music, but most of all he loved cock. It was a shock to me to find such a masculine man who was so captivated by cock and other men. He also seemed to be a magnet for men who shared the same interest. I got to know more about the men as I sat in the sun that long summer afternoon.

Max was Wolfie's oldest childhood friend. They were brought up together. Max's father worked for the Von Hellenburgs and both boys were unhappy. Max was despised because he was so small, Wolfgang because he was intelligent. The two boys became friends, companions and fellow sexual experimenters. The two boys discovered sex together. Max was a sex machine, always ready, always willing.

Professor Gottfried Von Schmidt discovered sex through Wolfie. Apparently it was love at first sight for him when he found the young Nordic God in his class. He admired Wolfgang from a distance for years. He was always a proper instructor and they finally got together only after Wolfie had joined the army and left the University.

Altenburg had joined the group as a result of his studies of sexual aberration. He had despised effeminacy as a grotesque perversion and studied it in order to define the sickness. He was an old friend of Von Schmidt's who came upon Wolfie and Gottfried in bed when visiting. He was shocked and appalled. He spent a night tossing and turning in distress at his friend's perversion. As the night progressed he discovered that in addition to his shock he was also stimulated and turned on. The next day he had his first experience with man sex. He became a convert.

Wertheimer was the odd man out in the group. He was very proper and correct. He was interested in sex but not to the extent of the other men. He was masculine but not as much as Wolfie, Max or the two professors. I didn't discover his role in the group until the next day.

Altenburg was my sexual guide. He was a man of science and a man who liked man sex. He told me that he made a study of it. It was a scientific study, he assured me. "But I will admit, that the field work is the best part," he joked. "I insist on trying everything I learn about. The problem is that the sexual capacities and capabilities of man are varied and erratic. What causes an orgasm in one man is disgusting or ineffectual in another."

"That must be disappointing." I said.

"Not at all. It is exciting," the professor said. "The how and why of the variation is my interest. Nothing is as expected."

"I must admit that my friend's detachment ends when he comes in contact with a man who excites him," Von Schmidt said. He was smiling. "Serious scientific study rarely involves lust!"

"Let me suggest that serious scientific study always involves passion!" Altenburg replied. "You don't devote your life to a study that merely interests you! I also think it is clear the sexual activity in plants and single cell creatures is entirely without lust and desire. The more advanced the animal to more important lust and desire become."

"Thus, Herr Professor," Samuel said, "the ultimate expression of humanity is unbridled lust and passion!" Everyone laughed.

"Would it were so!" Von Schmidt said. "But I do think you may have something there. It does seem that the role of physical attraction and the passion for sex increases as the animal is more advanced. Horses and cows have one level, monkeys and apes another and human beings the ultimate!"

"Did Darwin speak of this?" I asked. "My great aunt was appalled by Darwinian theories, but I had never found them objectionable. She was a firm believer that every word in the Bible was scientifically true. That was very hard for me as an archaeologist."

"To be able to select your partner is a remarkable breakthrough. Plants cannot select the pollen that pollinates them. We can, and thus we have evolved with greater speed." Altenburg said.

"I would be glad to have you pollinate me!" Max said. Everyone laughed. "But I won't have your babies! It would ruin my figure!"

"I think that may be a blow to your evolutionary theory. Where do we men who love other men fit in?" Wolfgang asked.

"That was my concern before I met you and Von Schmidt." Altenburg said.

"I think you mean before Wolfie's cock rammed your prostate for the first time!" Von Schmidt said. Everyone laughed, expecting the doctor to be embarrassed. He easily slipped into a formal professorial role as if he were lecturing his students. His formal style seemed at odds with the subject matter.

"Well," he said, "that was an inspiration I admit. I couldn't rectify the intense physical pleasure I experienced with Wolfgang with my concept of abject degeneracy and perversion."

"But you did, Herr Professor?" Samuel asked. Altenburg smiled.

"Of course I did!" the professor continued. "It wasn't just the physical pleasure I experienced. I was shocked at the complete lack of guilt I felt."

"I realized that Darwin's survival of the fittest often focuses on procreation as the central element of life. Survival however involves a wide range of activities, finding food, defending one's homes, sometimes finding new, safer better places to live. If we were purely focused on our mate and children, hunting is difficult, exploration all but impossible. It is the man who is less interested in his mate that can love the long hunting expedition. He can be the warrior who spends months and even years away from his home, protecting the frontier. For the man who loves his fellow man, this is no hardship."

"The father must be cautious so he can protect his wife and children. The single man can be bold. The single man can devote his life to science or religion or art and not be distracted by children and a demanding wife," he concluded.

"And the sex is the frosting on the cake!" Max interjected. Altenburg almost rolled on the ground laughing.

"Exactly!" he cried, still laughing. "Exactly. If the ecstasy of sexual intercourse was limited to men and women only, this would be a great discouragement to the solitary man or to the group of men who spend a week on a hunting expedition. Man sex is part of the order of the universe! It is an essential part of human evolution."

"We all have our own hands," Samuel added. "We can always masturbate."

"It's not the same as a man's mouth on your cock, or your cock in his ass!" Von Schmidt said.

"Truer words were never said!" I added. This was the first time I had been in a serious conversation about sex, not to mention man sex. I was intellectually stimulated; the ideas were new to me. I too felt the absence of guilt. My cock was non intellectually stimulated.

Altenburg looked at my enlarging cock with approval.

"It's dinner time. Who wants to help make dinner?" Wolfie asked. Despite Wolfie's obvious wealth there were no servants in the house. This was very usual even in post War Germany. The Kaiser was gone but the servants remained. At first, I thought Max was a servant, but he was a friend.

"I don't know how to cook, but I am more than willing to help someone who does," I said.

"If you don't mind expedition food, I'll give dinner a try," Samuel cried. "Follow me!" We went to the kitchen and found it well stocked. There were fresh vegetables from the local gardens and a pork roast. Samuel purported to be an amateur cook, but he seemed skilled to me.

"Did you learn to cook on an expedition?" I asked.

"I was blessed with a wonderful aunt," he explained. "My mother died when I was young and I was raised by her Aunt Sally. She was a firm believer in self reliance. "Wealth is no excuse for being helpless," she would say. "I can tell you it made me a popular guy in the trenches of France."

"I think it will make you a popular man here!" I said. He smiled.

"This is a very agreeable collection of men. I am half Jewish, and that is an impediment to friendship in some places. Not here."

"They are not very formal, by German standards." I said. "They seem to look at the man, not the rank or position in society. It is hard to believe that Professors would associate with students so informally." Samuel laughed.

"I think they evaluate a man by his cock!" he said. "Cocks are the great equalizer!"

"Size? Is that why I am here?" I asked.

"I don't think so," Samuel replied. "It seems to me that they like men who are willing to use their cocks for fun. As long as you are willing to play, they are happy. You fit well in the group. I wasn't so calm after my first visit here."

"I don't feel that calm." I said.

"You look calm," Samuel said. "I was a nervous wreck. Afraid of what might happen next, and afraid that it might not happen!" We both laughed.

"That describes me well," I was both afraid of the new things that might happen next and wanted them to happen. "How was it?"

"Well, let's say I have never looked back with regret," Samuel said. "I had thought that I was incapable of intense feelings. That, fortunately, was false. You'll know after dinner what it's like."

"What happens after dinner?"

"Let's say that after several bottles of wine, everyone lets their defenses down and becomes very open and receptive to new ideas." Samuel said. "Very open!"

"My god!" I said. "How much more open can you get?" He laughed.

"You will know soon enough!" He had me chopping up vegetables and fruits and some herbs. I had no vision of what he was making but after an hour of work dinner was ready. It was very good. Not elaborate, but good.

Dinner was indeed festive and fun. We were all well educated, articulate men and somewhat relaxed. Conversation flowed easily and was both clever and stimulating. By now I hardly noticed that we were all nude. After four bottles of wine the conversation returned to cocks. By that time we were all really interested.

"The penis is the ultimate symbol of man," Altenburg said, "but, it may not be the most sensitive part of a man's anatomy. Some men think their nipples are more sensitive. I tried to do a poll on it and wasn't able to get it distributed correctly."

"It's the cock head for me!" Max said.

"Prostate here," Von Schmidt said. "It can drive me crazy."

Wolfie joined the cock head camp, Max and Wertheimer joined the prostate group. It was a tie. "Jean, you need to vote to break the tie!" Altenburg cried. I couldn't have been more embarrassed.

"I hate to sound like a country bumpkin, but I don't know about what a prostate does or exactly where it is," I said.

"Well, this is your lucky day!" Von Schmidt said, laughing. "I will be glad to enlighten you."

"Education is your life! Always ready to help a student in need!" Max quipped.

"We all have something to teach Jean," Von Schmidt said. "Everyone should make an effort to give him a few pointers about the joys of man sex."

"I appreciate the thought, but I think I will learn at my own pace!" I said. I didn't want to be the focus of attention. The conversation moved on to other subjects and we left the table. The main room of the house was a large hall with the dining table at one end and sofas on the other. There was a large bay window on one side and a smaller bay on the other. I sat in the small bay while the dishes were cleared and washed. Max joined me.

He had been the first to suck me that morning, but I hadn't been with him since. "Enjoying yourself?" he asked.

"I certainly am," I replied. "But it's all new experiences to me."

"You really never did this before?" he asked. "Wolfie and I have been playing with each other since we were kids."

"It's new to me. It feels great but takes some getting used to."

"I loved sucking Wolfie from the start. The first time I did him he popped in my mouth. Some guys hate that. I thought it was milk. I was fifteen when I figured out it was sperm," Max said. "I was shocked when Wolfie sucked me. He says that I have the most cock like cock he's ever seen."

"What does that mean?" I asked. He parted the thick pubic bush and exposed his cock.

"My cock sits deep inside the skin. The skin's all wrinkled and hairy, the cock is veiny. The head is nice and big." He peeled back the skin and exposed his head. It was pink-purple with a wide slit. He was so hairy that it looked naked and exposed without the covering of hair. I slid over and began to suck him.

It wasn't what I expected at all. I knew that being sucked gave me a rush of excitement, but hadn't guessed that sucking was so exciting. I had been passive; it was doubly exciting to be active. Max responded immediately to my attention. The small cock lost in the hair was impressive when it reached full size. I wondered if it would ever stop.

As Max said, it wasn't a pretty cock, but it was all man meat and I loved it. I was lying sideways on a sofa and I felt tongue licking my cock. It was Von Schmidt. We rearranged ourselves so that we all could be more comfortable.

"Let me go. I don't want to shoot yet," Max said. I did and immediately rotated so that I could suck Von Schmidt. He had a thick, stubby bullet shaped cock. His head was covered in slimy goo, which briefly offended me. I didn't want to lick it, but he was a professor and I didn't want to offend him by getting ready to suck him, then rejecting him.

Later, I found out that Von Schmidt's nick name was the Creamery. He oozed more pre cum and shot more cum that any other man they knew. When my tongue touched the slime, I was all but intoxicated by his pre cum. His cock was thick and hard to deep throat, but every time I did, he oozed a bucket full of his pre cum. I soon figured out how coax out the wonderful fluid.

"Calm down," Wolfie said as he observed us. "Summer nights are very long. The professor never runs dry." I hadn't realized that Wolfie was watching. I got up and immediately sucked his cock. I was like a man dying of thirst who discovers water. I couldn't get enough of cock.

I was on my knees sucking Wolfie when Von Schmidt began poking his cock in my ass hole. "Relax and sit back," he said. Remarkably, I did and his monster eased into my ass. It was large, but heavily lubricated and I felt no pain at all. Technically he fucked me, but it was more like a slow occupation. I felt an explosion of feeling as I discovered where my prostate was.

I was oddly pleased the Professor was in my ass. He was a great man and he had chosen me. He was moaning some and sighed when I was fully impaled. He pumped slowly and as I got use to him I enjoyed it more.

Max scooted between Wolfie's legs to suck my cock. I began to shiver as I reached a climax and I popped. Wolfie began to shoot volley after volley of cum in my mouth. Von Schmidt began to jerk and I knew he was filling my ass with his cum. I was inordinately pleased this gifted man was sharing his seed, the fruit of his loins, with me.

CHAPTER 3

- *Dresden 1937* -

The weekend in the country did nothing but get better as the sexual atmosphere grew. Once I got used to having a cock in my ass hole my attitude toward sex changed. Of course I liked sex before, but I didn't have any idea that there was a level of feeling I hadn't even dreamed of. It was the first time I had ever lost myself in sexual pleasure. It was as if I was unconscious of any feelings other than sexual

Everyone there recognized the change. I tried to describe the feelings and I awoke the scientific instincts of the two professors. Altenburg thought that the pressure of the cock on my prostate must have let loose a flood of hormones. I wasn't sure, but whatever it was it was extraordinary.

That night in bed Von Schmidt and Altenburg alternated fucking and fingering my ass. Altenburg had two fingers in my ass, one on each side of my prostate. Von Schmidt watched me twitch and moan as his friend explored my sensitivities. When Altenburg got tired with this, Von Schmidt worked his cock in again.

"You see," Von Schmidt said. "No matter how good the professor's fingers are, they can't quite equal a man-cock. I don't know if it is the physical sensation or the intellectual knowledge that another man's most private organ is deep in your ass."

"I wonder if it is because you are brought up to see the ass as dirty and ugly, "Altenburg mused."When you have these spectacular feelings of pleasure, the contrast between the taboo and the sensation is so exciting." We heard some moaning from the next room and got up to see what was happening. Samuel was sitting on Wolfie's cock as Max worked his cock into the same hole.

Samuel had seemed so proper, but he was obviously enjoying the double fucking. I couldn't believe he could take two cocks. Looking at his face, I saw the same abandonment to sexual pleasure I had felt hours before. I knew what he was feeling and the excitement spread. Altenburg got behind me and slipped his cock in my love tunnel. Altenburg's cock was very different from Von Schmidt, but just as pleasurable.

Max began to moan as he popped. He pulled out and Wolfie motioned for me to replace him. My cock was large so I was worried, but Samuel looked really excited. I moved into Max's position and positioned my cock at ass. It didn't seem possible that Samuel could take both. We were the two biggest men there. Von Schmidt and Altenburg were really close and Von Schmidt coated my cock with some lubricant. I realized it was his cum. Altenburg had been stroking his cock and began to shoot his cum directly on my cock and Samuel's asshole. I felt a surge of passion and thrust, burying my cock in the tight ass.

Wolfie hadn't been completely hard, but his cock was long enough to remain in the hole. Once I was in, he began to moan and my cock was squeezed by his cock as it bloated. I was making small thrusts, massaging Wolfie's cock as he massaged Samuel's prostate. It was a good night at the country house.

I went back to Berlin the next day, but continued to see everyone periodically. I had to return to France at the end of the session and wasn't able to return to Berlin. Events conspired against me. I was off to the United States to the University of Pennsylvania to work on a major expedition. They needed a French-speaking archaeologist and my old professors had recommended me. It was a wonderful opportunity and for the next few years I was fully engaged in the expedition and its associated studies.

The collapse of the stock market in 1929 eventually dried up all the funding for the project and I returned to France and my father found me a position in the local museum. Fortunately for me the director, M. Adam, was interested in anthropology and we had the basic elements in our collection for a good exhibit on the pre history of our district. He actually was able to scrape together some money for excavations. One of these resulted in the discovery of some fine cave art. I became very familiar with the caves of our district. This knowledge was very useful to me later on.

I corresponded with most of my Berlin friends throughout this period. In 1937 I was invited to a celebration of Von Schmidt's 40th year as a professor. The event was to be a scholarly conference to take place in Dresden. I was a bit puzzled as to why it wasn't in Berlin, but I was asked to give a paper. I found that he was teaching there, and no one had mentioned that he had left Berlin.

The Director allowed me to present the results of my discoveries at the conference. I was surprised he didn't want me to present them in

Paris. He told me he wanted me to dazzle the Boche with my work. This I did.

This was my first visit to Dresden. Photographs didn't do justice to the fairy tale like architecture of the city. All of France was talking about the new stark architecture of modernism. I wallowed in the unbelievable architectural fantasies of the Electors of Saxony.

I got there on the morning of my lecture and didn't have time to do more than say hello to my friends. The conference was in the museum next to the Zwinger and my lecture was a great success. It was sensation. I had made beautiful photographic slides of the wall paintings and presented never seen before works.

Von Schmidt, Wolfie and Altenburg were effusive in their praise. They were busy until the conference was over the next day, but I was invited to Von Schmidt's house for the weekend. Wolfie winked at me when they mentioned this and I knew what was in store for me. I went to my hotel and found a note from a man named Samuel West, asking me to call on him.

I rang his room and a familiar voice answered. It was Wertheimer. I went over immediately to see him. He greeted me effusively and complemented me on the lecture.

"You drove the Nazi bastards crazy!" he said.

"What do you mean?" I asked. I hadn't seen any of the party officials there. There were uniformed men all over Germany and the atmosphere had changed dramatically since my stay there ten years before. There were no Brown Shirts at the conference.

"The prize winning lecture was to have been given by Otto Von Oldham on Aryan origins," Samuel said. "Your discoveries are dazzling. They were brilliant. They either give to prize to you, or embarrass themselves giving it to him." I hadn't realized that there was a prize.

"Did he find the Aryan origins?" I asked.

"Shit no!" Samuel said. "Bullshit wrapped in pompous and meaningless dribble!"

"Did you change your name?' I asked.

"Only here," he said. "I'm here trying to get some of my father's relatives out. It's bad to be a Jew here now. The Foreign Office thought I might be better if I had a non-Jewish name." I had no doubt that was true, but I also knew that Samuel must have been deep into the confidence of His Majesties' Government to get a passport with a false name on it. I certainly wasn't going to ask him any more questions on his new name. We had a nice conversation catching up on old times. Samuel told me he was teaching at Oxford and most of his studies took him to Central Europe. He said that he would be at Von Schmidt's after the conference ended.

We went downstairs and had a drink at the bar. A man came up to me and introduced himself as Fritz Dahlen, a local scholar. He had seen my lecture and was effusive in his praise. I caught Samuel looking at him in a strange way.

Samuel excused himself and Fritz asked me for dinner in the hotel dining room. I couldn't think of any reason to refuse so we had diner. Fritz was a genuine scholar of prehistory, and seemed like a nice man. His admiration for my discovery was unforced and genuine.

"If only it were in Germany, it would be perfect," he said. I don't think he realized how stupid it was to say that.

"Do you think the Rosetta stone would be better if it were found in Munich?" I asked. Fritz thought for a minute, and then roared in laughter.

"And the Stonehenge would be beautiful in downtown Berlin!" He laughed again. Fritz had dark, short hair, cut short the stood up straight, and a bristly mustache. He looked like an outdoors man, with a ruddy completion and clear, light blue eyes. He reminded me of Teddy Roosevelt, very vigorous and enthusiastic. His knee touched mine under the table several times and he didn't move it.

He suggested that we might go to a club he knew for a drink and a taste of the local nightlife. We went off but the café was closed so we stopped at his apartment for a nightcap. We went in a small door on a side street and up a steep flight of stairs. The minute I was inside the door of his apartment I realized the Fritz was a wealthy man. It was luxuriously furnished with old furniture and art work. The theme of the art work was Hercules, and other ancient heroes. There was no trace of Venus or Helen or Athena.

I recognized the sculptors of several of the works, and complemented him on his tastes. He brought out some very expensive English whiskey.

"Thank you," he said, "the sculptures are well known, but it is hard to find high quality copies."

"Am I mistaken that several are not copies?" I asked. He smiled.

"You do have a good eye. Several are original casts. My favorite is the Farnese Hercules. It is a copy in miniature," he said. "Roman, but obviously done by a skilled Greek artisan." He pointed to a muscular figure in bronze.

"I have always admired the statue, but I had a professor who claimed it was unnatural," I said. "He claimed that no man could be that muscular. I think he admired the Apollo Belvedere."

"I've always thought the Apollo was effeminate. I prefer the more masculine Hercules," Fritz said. "And I can prove him wrong on the unnatural musculature of the Hercules. Men can achieve that level of physical development."

"If they can, I would love to see it," I said. He sat next to me on a small couch.

"Actually, I have been working on it myself," Fritz said. "It has taken a lot work but I have almost recreated the look." He looked at me. "Feel my arms." Fritz flexed his biceps and I felt it. He was hard as a rock. I complemented him. I knew where we were heading and was interested.

"Very impressive," I said. I paused a second or two. "I would love to see the rest of you." He looked at me and smiled. After fixing me another drink he vanished into his bedroom. He returned stripped half naked. Fritz was magnificent. He had a spectacular sculptural physique with each muscle defined and clearly delineated. I am afraid that my admiration was clear and Fritz glowed in pleasure.

He posed and evoked all of the stances of ancient sculptural masterpieces. He obviously enjoyed my admiration. He was wearing a loincloth that slipped off after a few seconds and he was completely nude. He had the compact balls and cock of the Greek original. He had an evenly hairy chest; it must have been shaved at one time and was growing back. He stopped and sat next to me.

"Forgive me please," he said. "I have been working on my physique so long, but I never get to show it off. I must be boring you."

"Not at all," I said. His knee was touching mine again. "How did you do it?" "Let me show you my gym!" he said. He sounded like a little boy showing off his new toy. We got up and went to the next room. It was a small space, but was filled equipment. Some were barbells and similar implements; others were new inventions that looked a bit like Frankenstein's laboratory.

"Would you like to try one of my machines out?"

I didn't want to, but I wanted to be polite. "Take your clothes off," he instructed me. "The equipment is sweat stained and you might ruin them." I was sure that he wasn't worried about my clothes. I stripped and felt embarrassed at my comparatively scrawny body. Fritz wasn't too interested in my body. My cock was a different story all together.

As I folded my pants and dropped my shorts I turned to face him. He looked me over, smiled when he saw my cock and dropped to his knees and swallowed it whole. I wasn't soft, but wasn't hard either and it was a mouthful. Fritz loved it. I finally got him into a 69 position and licked his cock. He immediately shot a volley of cum as my lips caressed his head. Fritz had a beautifully formed cock and balls, genuinely Greek sculpture like, with good sized balls and nice cock. I discovered Fritz was a size queen and longed for big meat.

I assumed that when he shot off he would stop sucking me, but he continued and then got on his hands and knees and spread his ass. It was hard to believe the muscular god was twitching his ass at me in invitation. I was ripe and willing, but we had no lubricant.

Fritz wanted to be fucked dry so he could feel it more, he said. I coated my cock with spit and worked it in. He looked like Hercules and his ass was muscle bound and tight. He was a wonderful bottom. He wiggled and twisted to try to manipulate my cock and get it into the right places. In spite of his masculine appearance he wanted to be used. I spent the night with him and dropped three or four loads in his ass or mouth. It was a great night.

I got back to my room in time to get dressed for the next day's meetings. As predicted my lecture wasn't mentioned in the newspapers, in spite of the generous coverage of the event. Brown Shirts were everywhere on the second day, and the lecture hall was filled for Otto Von Oldham's lecture.

As Samuel had predicted, it was shit wrapped in pompous verbosity. There were no facts or discoveries or understandings. Von Oldham was presented with flowers by little girls at the end of his speech. He did receive a prize for the most distinguished lecture, presented by Von Schmidt himself.

At a reception following the seminars Von Schmidt avoided me. Most of the people at the reception had clustered around Von Oldham so I got to spend some time with old friends I hadn't seen since Berlin ten years earlier. I saw Fritz beside Von Oldham several times. After a while Wolfie came over to me.

"I can't tell you how embarrassed Von Schmidt is," Wolfie whispered. "This is the final humiliation for him. He is trying to get out of Germany, and this was the only way he could get away. It's too dangerous for him here now." I nodded. Things were much worse in Germany than I had thought. Of course I knew it was bad for Jews, but Von Schmidt was as German as they come. "Please come to the house after," Wolfie asked. "He does want to see you and apologize."

"I'm looking forward to it," I said. "And tell the professor that there is no need to apologize. These are difficult times. We must do what we need to do." Wolfie looked relieved and returned to the professor.

When the crowd began to dissipate, I went over to Von Oldham to congratulate him on winning the prize. I didn't want to seem as if I was disappointed. My father always said that conventional politeness could drive your enemies crazy, and I decided to adopt his theory.

He thanked me. "I am so sorry that I missed your lecture yesterday, I was doing last minute polishing. My student, Fritz, told me it was superb," Otto said. "I long to get back in the field again. I have been trapped in my academic pursuits too much lately."

"There is so much excitement in new finds," I said. He nodded politely and turned to accept the congratulations of a Nazi party official.

Max was waiting at my hotel to take me to Von Schmidt's home. I was to spend the rest of my stay there he said and he had packed my clothes and paid my bill at the hotel. I hadn't planned on this, but it did save money and I knew that my Director had difficulty funding my trip. We drove in his expensive car into an equally expensive suburb.

The house was beautiful, very grand and expansive. I found out it had been the home of the Lindeman family who had been forced to leave. They all but gave it to Von Schmidt to insure it didn't fall into Nazi hands.

"Your lecture was brilliant!" Von Schmidt said as he saw me and gave me a big bear hug. "Just Brilliant! If I had realized it was going to be half as good as it was I would have not invited you. I deserved a greater prize than I could give!" He led me into the spacious home. Max and Wolfie were there as was Altenburg and several men I didn't know.

"Jean, I would like you to meet some new friends of ours," Gottfried said. "This is Hans van der Luft of the University of Utrecht, and Bruno Silvano of the University of Padua. All were archaeologists and members of our fraternity." We shook hands. Hans was tall and thin, bald and had a mustache. Bruno was short and stocky, with curly black hair and a beard to match. Hans was blond and had an extraordinarily pale complexion and Bruno was heavily tanned. The two were physical opposites.

"And you know Samuel West, from Oxford," Von Schmidt continued. I shook hands with Sam as if I hadn't known him for years. Max had made a good dinner and there was good wine, whisky and beer. Gottfried wanted to cover all of the alcoholic tastes of his guests.

CHAPTER 4

- *The War Begins* -

The party at Professor Schmidt's house became quite festive once everyone had apologized and the apologies were accepted. I did not feel wronged and so I could be very generous in my protestations that it was all right for me. Part of the problem was the German sense of propriety. I knew the Germans were very competitive. They wanted to be the best scholars in the world. Some knew you couldn't do that if you only won rigged competitions.

Bruno, the Italian archaeologist, was living in an archaeologist dream. Il Duce was pouring money into excavations and reconstruction. Bruno was a reasonable man and I don't think he was a fascist. I wondered how I would react if I were confronted by the dream job of a lifetime, offered to me by a dictator I despised. Hans van der Luft, the Dutch archaeologist and I had no need to worry about that. I had a brief vision of the President of France, or Queen Wilhelmina in military garb addressing a great throng of jackbooted followers and I knew we were safe.

We began to discuss the concept of the "master race" and had considerable fun at Herr Hitler's expense. This conversation was greatly enhanced by the professor's generous approach to drink. Bruno claimed to be the ultimate Italian, short, swarthy, hairy and horny. We agreed Wolfie looked like the perfect German. He claimed to have the Grossdeutcherdick, the prefect cock for the Gross Deutches Reich.

"I have heard that Herr Hitler has a dicklet and only has one ball," Van der Luft said. "Some say he may be trying to conquer the world to find his missing ball!" There was general laughter.

"Would the world be a better place if Hitler had Wolfie's cock?" Professor Schmidt asked. "What if our dictator had Jean's meat?" There was another outbreak of laughter.

"I know our friend Jean is merely a degenerate Frenchman, but he has Le Grande Cocque Francaise!" Wolfie said almost choking in laughter. "I'd rather be fucked by a mere Frenchman with a donkey dong, than a mini-dicked, mono-balled dictator."

"We in the Netherlands are modest and small, but I can assure you if there is a hole in a dike near me, I will fuck it closed, not plug it with my finger!" Hans added. "Dutch dicks do dikes! The "master race" may be made of supermen, but give me super cocks!" To illustrate his point, Hans unbuttoned his pants and exposed his cock. It was an anatomical wonder. It must have flopped halfway to his knees.

"That looks like something Mae West could use as a boa!" Bruno exclaimed.

"She should be so lucky!" Wolfie said. "Shit, I should be so lucky!" Everyone laughed.

"Well. If anyone wants to play leaking dike, I am willing to plug them," Hans said. At that moment Max appeared, completely naked except for a formal bow tie. He must have been working out, because he looked more muscular than he had ten years earlier, but was just as hairy.

"Let me be first in line!" he said. Two seconds later it seemed as if everyone in the room was naked and sucking. The room exploded into sex. I found Bruno sucking my cock while I sucked the Professor's cock. Otto was a leaker and I had thought often about his dick dribbling its creamy man juice. If anything, it had grown creamier and richer as he aged. With one taste, it seemed as if ten years apart had vanished.

Bruno was a cock hound. I had heard Mediterranean men were macho and hard to entice into homosexual play. Bruno spent the next several hours on his hands and knees sucking any cock within range. He loved cock, but was happy serving rather than being served.

The shy and unassuming Dutchman, Hans, was anything but shy when he was nude and erect. He was the cockmaster, picking his partners for his pleasure. He said straight out he had no interest in the feelings of his partners. He wanted to exercise his cock and anyone who wanted to try it, would have to take what he could get.

With Hans' monster cock, he was accustomed to picking and choosing his partners and doing what he wanted. I have no interest in sado-masochistic games, but that wasn't what Hans wanted either. Hans wanted to fuck ass at full speed. Nothing soft and caring, just man fucking. Max wanted that too. They put on a good show.

Not only was Hans huge, he had the opposite of a hair trigger. He stayed hard, but had no drive to shoot. He said he was a local, not an express train. "If you take a ride, it's going to be a long one," Hans said. Max lasted fifteen minutes before he was exhausted at the rigorous shafting and he got off.

Much to my surprise, Otto was next in line. In my experience the old professor was a top, but he got on his back and opened his ass wide for Hans. After a while Hans needed a rest and he signaled to me to replace him. He pulled out and I slid in Otto's quivering hole. At first it was odd to have my cock in my former professor's warm ass. He had fucked me many times and there was an odd sense of impropriety. This was a turn on. I realized I was living the student's fantasy, fucking his professor. Otto moaned in pleasure and we enjoyed it.

By now Bruno was sucking Samuel, and wiggling his ass in the air. The Italian had spread his cheeks, so his pink ass hole with its little rosebud could be seen in the mass of swirling black hair covering his ass. Wolfie saw it too. He popped his cock in the hole and he and Samuel kissed as they fucked Bruno from opposite ends.

I watched them and soon realized it was a mistake. I can control my orgasms as long as I work at it. When I feel as if I am going to shoot, I can slow down and hold it off. Every time I get near to shooting and hold back makes it harder to get to the point of shooting again, so I build up a load of cum that can't get released. It's a spectacular feeling to have a full load trapped in your balls. My ultra sensitive cock gets almost raw it is so stimulated, but I still don't reach the point of ejaculating. I love the feeling you get a second before you shoot and had found ways to make it last for minutes.

Watching Wolfie, Bruno and Samuel made me lose my concentration and I shot off. I pulled out of Otto's ass a second before and ejaculated sperm ten feet across the room. Max and von Altenburg were watching and applauded. I was spent, but Otto rolled me over into the 69 position and began to suck me. I was too tired to suck him, but I did lick his dripping cock. That was enough to turn me on again and discovered I wasn't too tired. We sucked until we could shoot again.

I must have fallen asleep around two in the morning. At dawn I woke and found Otto and Von Altenburg in bed with me. I could hear Samuel moaning in another room. He was on Hans' cock and was obviously enjoying his ride. When I moved, Otto responded by working his cock into my ass.

I remembered the "lesson" in Wolfie's country house. Otto's dick massaged my ass and prostate. It was a massage, rather than being fucked. When he got too close to shooting, he turned me over to Altenburg, who slipped into my tender hole. It was both friendly and erotic. The sex had been non-stop, as if this was our last chance, as if there was no tomorrow. I said this to Otto.

"I don't know if there is a tomorrow. I have little hope," Otto said. "In a century of hard work Germany created a brilliant university system and had a spectacular cultural flowering. Beethoven, Wager, Bruckner, Strauss composed. German physicists, archaeologists, and science seemed to dazzle the world. In four years almost nothing is left. How could one small man destroy so much?"

"Hitler may pass," Altenburg said. He caressed my prostate with his cock. "It may not be that bad. People will come to their senses."

"You are an optimist," Otto replied. "I think it could take a century to recover what we have lost. I think no one will come to their senses until it is too late," I was going to say something, but was feeling so mellow I just relaxed and let the two men enjoy my ass. A half hour later Altenburg popped and I shot. Otto took my load.

I had to get back to France and I left that morning. It had been an odd visit. I was worried for my friends; I sensed they were in danger. I also had experienced the most intense sexual feelings in a decade. Ecstasy mixed with anxiety is a peculiar feeling. I never guessed this would be typical of my future life experiences.

CHAPTER 5

- France 1940 -

It was hard to believe the entire military might of the French Republic could crumble and collapse in the short period following the Nazi invasions of Belgium and the Netherlands. I wouldn't say my respect for the government was as great as some thought, but in my most cynical moments I couldn't have believed France could have collapsed so totally.

My Department was untouched directly by the war, but was assigned to the German zone of occupation. An automobile accident a year earlier had left me lame and unfit for service in the army, so when the Germans arrived, I was one of the few able bodied men in the community. I was also the Acting Director of the local museum. Like my father, M. Adam was on active duty and we didn't know if he had been captured, or escaped.

The Mayor, M. Auguste, Bishop DesJardins and I were selected as a reception committee to meet our occupiers as they entered the city. My German language skills were needed, which is why I was selected to be a part of this distinguished group. We met the Germans on the edge of the city and officially surrendered the city. An hour later, they were ensconced at the Hotel Metropolitan, the best hotel in town.

We surrendered to the vanguard of the occupying troops. A junior officer told me to report to the Hotel at nine the next morning, to work out the details of the civil administration. I arrived at the hotel and was taken to the Royal Suite. The Royal Suite was by no means as grand as its name, but it was the best the hotel had to offer.

An intimidating officer entered the room. He was almost a cinema's version of a German officer and it took me a few seconds to realize it was Wolfie. He was now a major in the Wermacht. I was speechless as the junior officer who brought me there was dismissed.

"Jean, it is so good to see you," Wolfie said warmly after the corporal left the room. "Even under these difficult circumstances, it is good."

"How did you end up here?" I asked.

"It's awful at home. At least I don't need to kill anyone in the Civil Administration office," he said.

"You are in charge?" I asked.

"Officially," he answered. "The army still has some authority. The Nazi operatives and the Gestapo are the true power in Germany today. I am here on good behavior. I don't think they trust me, or some other members of the officer corps for that matter, but we all seem to suffer from our Prussian upbringing. We all obey."

"I wish that I could be so pleased to see you," I said.

"I don't think it is a good idea for anyone to know we are friends," Wolfie said. "If you can help me, I can help you."

"I could never betray France," I said.

"Nor could I betray my homeland, but I won't be a party to evil. The Nazi's are scum, filth," Wolfie said. "I am little more than a figurehead here. The Gestapo gives me orders. I am officially in charge. Where I can help, I will. I can at least give you advance information."

"What is their plan for us?" I asked.

"Some of them are mad dogs. There is no way to tell," Wolfie said. "I'm not trusted; they don't like the sons of the aristocracy. I do hear things and I command the troops. They can't do much without me," Wolfie smiled. "I have developed a reputation of indolence. I am here because the area has no real significance. It is an ideal place for a lazy bastard like me! Don't let anyone know you know me. As a translator you are invaluable, no one will think anything of your coming here."

"Who is in charge?"

"Tuefelman is the Gestapo officer for this region. I think he is a sadist. He had a horrible reputation in Berlin."

"You knew him?

"Only by reputation. I was never interested in the Sado-masochist games some liked. Max knew him and didn't like him."

"Where is Max?" I asked. Wolfie laughed.

"He is still my servant. Officers live well in the new Germany. It is a lot better to be doing an old friend's laundry than to be fighting on the front line," Wolfie replied.

"There doesn't seem to have been that much fighting for any of you," I said with some bitterness in my voice.

"I'm afraid for Germany. I don't think the Brits will give up and where the British are the Americans will be," Wolfie said. "The Nazis are monsters. The British would never accept them. You need to go before the spies get suspicious. Max will contact you if I need to talk." We shook hands and I left.

For the first several months little changed. There were shortages of almost everything, but we were in a rural area with many farms. My father had not been found yet. He apparently wasn't a prisoner of war, but they hadn't found his body either. My mother was brave, but lost a lot of weight. My Aunt Elise came from Paris to stay with us and take care of my mother.

I ran the museum and served as the town translator for both the French and the Germans. Curiously, the Germans seemed to regard me as a neutral conduit of language, not a real person. This proved to be very advantageous for the town and me. I received a letter at the Museum from a Swiss man, Herr S. Westburg, informing me a friend of his had seen my father in London wearing the cross of Loraine.

He was alive and with DeGaul. My mother stopped dying. My Aunt felt she should join him. She reasoned that if my father was with DeGaul there might be reprisals and my mother would be better off in London, or at least Switzerland. I went to see Wolfie and he made out the correct papers. He told me my Aunt was a perceptive woman. As I left, he asked if there were any Jews in the town. I, of course, said no.

"That is very lucky for them," he said. Wolfie was clever. I knew exactly what he meant. That night, my Aunt and mother called on Dr. Dreyfuss and had them move into a vacant farm we owned a few kilometers from town. I went to their son's apartment and got him into the attic of the museum until I could find a safe place.

The museum was still open to the public and it wasn't an ideal hiding place. I had spent much of the last decade looking for cave paintings and I realized that I had a near complete knowledge of the underground geology of the area. For years I was annoyed no one would join me on my rambles. Suddenly I realized this was near miraculous good fortune.

I moved Louis Dreyfuss to the Blue Bear Cave. It was big, complex and hidden from view. It was also completely unknown. I left him there with a week of food, returned to town and destroyed my notes about the caves. Ten years of research went up in smoke.

Wolfie had given me transit papers for two people, my aunt and mother, but it did not mention their names or sex. Dr. and Mme Dreyfus used them. My mother crossed at a cousin's farm on the Swiss border. Much to my surprise my aunt returned and did not escape. She told me women could do things that men can't in wartime.

Louis got out a week later using the same farm. I wrote Herr Westburg to tell him of a package coming his way. A month later I learned my Mother and Louis were in London.

Max had become a messenger. Wolfie was very suspect, but respectable, so they used him as a front man when they needed a presentable man to represent Germany. In a stunning failure, the Gestapo never found out Wolfie could speak French. His school records showed he had studied English and Italian. He learned French from a childhood tutor.

Wolfe's official translator was a Gestapo agent who had no command of idiomatic French at all. Wolfie was to go to Switzerland to help negotiate sealing the border more tightly and when his commander heard the translator try to make a French sentence, the man was dismissed on the spot. The commander, General Wildebrandt, could speak some French and didn't want to be humiliated in front of the Swiss officials. His rank gave him power, even with the Gestapo. I was drafted to be a translator for the visit, until they could find another.

The General, Wolfie and I were off to Switzerland for a week of discussions. The General seemed to be a pleasant man once you got to know him. In peacetime, he had been assigned to an embassy as an aide, and he had no desire to get back into fighting. It was obvious he was glad to be out of the war.

It was clear Wildebrandt had no interest in closing up the border at all. He was a clever man and I knew he would have no trouble writing a report that made things sound good to his superiors, but the negotiations were an excuse to get away from the stress of occupied France. I had a day off when the General and Wolfie went to the embassy in Bern and I decided to locate S. Westburg, my correspondent in Switzerland. His address was in Geneva.

I wanted to thank him for his help. I also wanted to check him out. I had read novels about double agents who allow small fry to escape to establish credibility and wanted to see the man in person and make sure he wasn't working out of the German Consul's office.

The office was easy to find, the sign over the door said it was the headquarters of the Beaux Arts Importers. The secretary called Herr Westburg and much to my surprise, Samuel Wertheimer appeared.

"Jean! You escaped!" he cried as he ushered me into his office. "Are you hurt?" I had all but forgotten about the accident and my bad leg, they seemed minor compared to the current disaster. I filled Sam in on the last few years and then explained my odd reason for being in Switzerland.

"My God, Jean! I can't believe you are here. A translator for the Germans! It's too bad you got out. A man in that position could be very useful to us."

"When I saw you in Dresden I knew you were working for the King. I am just here for a day. I will be going back this weekend." Sam didn't need to recruit me to help, I was ready. He hadn't realized Wolfie was in charge of the area, and knew of General Wildebrandt.

"Your General likes men!" Samuel said. "He was in Britain at the Embassy and cut a wide swath in some circles. He was good at cocktail parties and pleasant company for the ladies, but his real interest was athletes and weight lifters. No wonder he is with Wolfie."

"I'm no athlete, so you're out of luck there," I said. "I'll be no lame Mata Hari for you!" We both laughed. I was heavily bearded now and had put on some weight so I was as far from a svelte sex kitten as any human being could be. The combination of images was comic.

"The General likes weight lifters, but he also likes men who are big in another sense!" Samuel explained. "Your accident didn't effect that did it?" I laughed.

"Not at all. Everything is still working. It is a bit rusty from lack of use."

"Well, if the opportunity arises, follow Queen Victoria's advice to her Daughter as she married the German Crown Prince. Close your eyes and think of England!" he said, and then he paused. "Oh, and don't forget to take notes."

"Sam, we've moved on from Mata Hari to Queen Victoria. Somehow I don't see myself in either role." We both laughed.

"I will get you a radio so we can communicate. Sometimes, I need something specific." He looked at me. "You do realize how dangerous this is?" I was surprised that being recruited to be a spy was so easy. Samuel and I said almost nothing. We both knew what was needed and had to be done.

"I'm afraid I do," I said. We kissed and I returned to my hotel. I got back before the General and Wolfie returned. They called me to their suite. The meeting at the embassy had not been a success. Both men had been through the ringer. Their scheme was to do as little as possible without having attention drawn to them, but they had miscalculated. Room service brought a bottle of English whiskey and they sat down to figure out a scheme to keep from being transferred to a place that might see some action.

I was part of the discussions. The General had no problem with escapees. He wasn't anti-Semitic and seemed to like the French. He didn't want anything to happen to his men, but other than that he didn't care.

I went to the bathroom, and was pissing when the General appeared. I had drunk a lot and had a full bladder. The General watched. I was embarrassed until I realized he was all but drooling. He stood beside me and held my cock as I pissed.

"It's beautiful," he said quietly. "Big and beautiful."

CHAPTER 6

- The Blue Bear Cave, 1941 -

I was in the bath when the General came in and stared at my cock. It was hard to piss in his gaze. He solved that problem by deciding to suck me while I pissed. I had never been into water sports, but I found myself turned on by the General's efforts to coax the golden liquid from my cock. He wasn't shy or embarrassed or concerned. It was pure cock passion and he was filled cock lust.

The General was childlike as he swallowed the last of my piss. It was as if I had given him a special gift. I later found he liked everything that spurts from the cock. He didn't care if it was cum, precum or piss. When I finished pissing he got up.

"I can't tell you how much I want to have sex with you," he said. "Let's get naked and play."

"What about Von Hellenburg?" I asked. I didn't want him to know I knew Wolfie as well as I did.

"He's a member of the Brotherhood," General Wildebrandt answered. "He's well hung. Not as good as you, but it's beautifully formed. It is the cock of a Greek god."

"Would that be a Teutonic God? I asked.

"I'm so sick of German this and German that I could puke," he responded. "I love the fatherland but there is a limit."

"I will bet German cock isn't one of the things you are sick of," I said. He winked at me and then burst out laughing.

"You understand me well enough!"

I had joked about my career as a Mata Hari like spy with Samuel, but it only took a few minutes to realize I was General Wildebrandt's idea of a sex kitten. I knew he liked body builders and athletes, but he liked big cocks even more. He wasn't my idea of the man of my dreams but he was a nice man, and good company.

The General was a bit over weight and moderately hairy. His cock was average, but his balls we monstrous. He had been in a sexual drought for the last several months. He had found it difficult to indulge his sexual interests with the Gestapo sharing the same building. He knew they had a file on him and knew his preferences, but he didn't want to give them any extra evidence to use against him. I realized that was why he was so interested in having sex with a Frenchman. He thought it unlikely that I would be connected with the arch-enemy, the Gestapo

When I sucked him, I briefly thought he was feeding me his own piss, but immediately realized that it was precum. The sweet liquid flowed from his cock in a constant stream. I thought it was constant during all sexual activity until I poked a finger in his ass and rammed his prostate.

I had never encountered a burst of precum that approached the force of an ejaculation before my experiences with the General. In him the walnut sized gland was the size of an apricot. I asked him if it was healthy. It was so large I thought it might be the result of a tumor. He told me doctors had checked him. The gland was big to match the balls.

"If only the cock matched the balls!" he complained. "My life would be perfect." The stubby, fat cock was rock hard but small enough to deep throat without choking. I told him the cock was a good size to play with. Wolfie walked in the bathroom.

"I wondered what could be keeping you two!" he said, laughing. "I should have realized that Mein General was up to his old tricks!" Wolfie was undressing to join us.

"Wolfchen! You know I have always done everything I could to promote friendship with our neighbors," the General said. "The war won't last forever and we will need friends afterwards." Wolfie laughed again.

"I appreciate that! If they ever give a Nobel Prize for the man fucked by the most men of different nationalities, I will nominate you. Peace through homosexual intercourse!" Wolfie proclaimed. "If you don't mind my French friend, if you could rearrange yourself so that you could suck Mein General while I fuck him, I would greatly appreciate it." I did as they suggested. The General obediently bent over so that Wolfie could more easily enter his ass.

"Be careful my friend. When I thrust, the cock ooze approaches flood level," Wolfie added. "They say Wagner originally envisioned the Rhine maidens swimming in the General's lust juice!" The General liked the comment and bellowed in laughter. Wolfie rammed him mid bellow and I almost choked. Every movement of Wolfie's cock in the love chute was reflected in the General's cock and the river of precum flowing from it.

I had never tasted a man being fucked before, but I was close to sharing each thrust with the two fucking men. I knew exactly where Wolfie's cock was at each moment. There was a brief burst when the cock head popped through the sphincter, followed by an even drool as the shaft followed. There was an orgasmic explosion when the head hit the prostate, then a thick, even flow until the shaft was fully enveloped in the chute.

I stopped Wolfie's methodical and even fucking when I wanted to get more precum. Wolfie rubbed his bloated head across the prostate several times and the General was crying in ecstasy.

"Stop, stop! I can't take it!" he cried. Wolfie wasn't a considerate man. He clearly liked having the General in his power. After toying with the General, Wolfie pulled out.

"It time for the main attraction. It's time for French cock!" he proclaimed. We changed positions. "Now General, do you want to show the Frenchman how a German General shoots his load, or do you want your best friend to wash his dinner down with your seed?" Wolfie asked. I chuckled at the thought. I took it as a rhetorical question but Wildebrandt seemed to take it seriously. I realized that the General was embarrassed by his cock but proud of his seed. While he was considering his answer I shoved my cock in his hole in a single thrust to the hilt.

Wolfie deep throated his as soon as I was fully lodged. The general's ass was tighter than I expected after Wolfie's long fuck session. The tunnel was hot and juicy, but tight fitting like an expensive glove. The General moaned in pleasure. I pulled out and shoved it in slowly the next time. This time I felt his prostate and paused there, caressing the organ as Wolfie had done before. Wolfie sports an impressive display of manhood, but mine was longer and thicker. I was also about as hard as I ever had been. When my bloated cock head touched the General's stimulated and abused prostate, he began to growl.

It was a deep guttural growling that seemed to be generated deep in his body. To this day I think that there is a connection between the prostate and the vocal chords. Wildebrandt's normal speaking voice was a tenor. His prostate's voice was a bass-baritone. I felt as if my cock was a bow and his prostate was the strings of a sexual bass. I grabbed his tits and pinched them. The tone dropped an octave.

I was half way through playing the Marseilles on his prostate when his entire rectum contracted. The prostate turned into a rock squeezing my cock as it passed. The General had an orgasm that was close to being a seizure. Wolfie took a couple shots then got out of the way and let the sperm fly all over the room. I would normally admire the display, but I had a distractingly intense and enjoyable orgasm myself. Remarkably my ejaculations alternated with his. His ass contracted before each of his shots and I felt as if he was milking me.

General Wildebrandt eventually introduced me to a sub culture of the Wermacht. It was included several cultured and aristocratic officers as well as working class enlisted men. The enlisted men were typically, big, muscular and athletic. All were interested in man sex, but none more than the General himself.

He was anti-Nazi, but weak. His only real form of protest was to under achieve, thus he was kept away from places were real soldiers were needed. With the manpower shortages characteristic of a single nation which decided to invade the world, the General was needed to hold this place in this part of France even if he didn't do it well. Wildebrandt had a good sense of self preservation but as long as none of his men got hurt, he was unconcerned by the activities of the French Resistance. After this play filled weekend in Bern, we returned home.

I was never a part of the organized Resistance. The only contact I had with the main group was through the Museum of Man in Paris. It was France's greatest anthropological institution and was a center of anti-Nazi activities. M. Albert D'Alan was my contact there. He always said he was the assistant to the assistant to. Albert was a classic low level bureaucrat that no one would ever pay any attention to, certainly no one in the German Master Race.

Albert was 45, of average height with thinning, mouse brown hair and he was dumpy. He had a droopy mustache that made him look a bit like a Basset Hound. We met three years earlier at a conference in Paris. Our actual meeting took place in the men's toilet at the urinal trough. He admired mine, and I admired his. The dumpy man had a donkey dong, graceless, but thick and meaty.

We got together after the conference at his apartment. He was slyly humorous in the satirical, world-weary way Parisians like to affect. We weren't much attracted to each other, but were sexually compatible. It was great sex with no strings attached. Intense, fun, very enjoyable, but meaningless. Needless to say, we made an effort to get together as regularly as possible.

I was in Paris in March 1942 at a meeting at the Museum for regional directors and he asked me to have dinner with him. I readily agreed. Food was beginning to become scarce even then, but Albert was a skillful cook and you wouldn't have guessed there was a problem. He said he had been talking to a Swiss art dealer, Herr Westburg, about selling some duplicate items from the collections.

"As you well know, we have far more items than we could ever use or need," Albert said. "Herr Westburg said that he had buyers, but that it was impossible to get them across the border. The German Guards seem to take a portion of all the items. They usually claimed they were objects which had belonged to Jews, and thus belonged to the Reich. Herr Westburg said you might have some thoughts on... transport."

"Small objects are no real problem," I said. "I must confess that smuggling across the border is second nature to many of the farmers of the district."

"Some of these objects might be quite large," Albert replied. "The size of a man." I had drunk several glasses of wine, and I just then realized what he was talking about. I laughed.

"That can be done."

"Very good. Is there a place to store these items until transport can be arranged?" he asked.

"My research into early cave paintings was very successful as you recall," I answered. "I think there are several good, safe and secure places. As far as I know, I am the only one to find them. You could be hidden there for years, if there was food. Even in our farming region, food could be a problem."

"Herr Westburg is a friend of yours?" Albert asked.

"He is an old friend," I said, "and a member of our fraternity."

"All of our communications have been by post so he is exceedingly careful and guarded in his letters. I take it you are working with him?"

"I do what I can," I replied. "I am a true son of France."

"M. Petain thinks the same, I am afraid," Albert said with great bitterness. "If we are betrayed it will more likely be a Frenchman than a German."

"I would not be that Frenchman," I said. "What do you want me to do?"

"We need to get people and information out of the country to the Free French authorities. The route through Spain is difficult; we need additional escape routes to Switzerland. We also need safe places to stay along the way," he explained. "Can you help?" I agreed of course. Albert said he would arrange to have an inspection visit to my museum in a week or so. The Director of the Museum of Man would arrange that. He would look over my sites and see if it would be useful.

I suddenly had a chill foreboding. What if Albert was an agent of the Vichy or the Germans? I was ready to go back to my hotel and he asked me to have another drink in the library. His apartment was small, and he led me to his wine cabinet. The cabinet opened to reveal another room. He flicked on a switch and I saw a small printing press.

"Did you know my father was a printer?" he asked. "I used to set type as a boy." On the walls were copies of the underground newspaper "Victoire!" It was a sensation in Paris since it carried the news from the BBC as well as letters from DeGaul. "I swore I would never set type again, but here I am working every night."

"It is very dangerous," I said. "They will shoot you!" I felt a wave of relief to know that Albert was a leader in the underground.

"I don't want to shock you," he said, "but they probably would shoot you too!" He laughed. "We are lucky. As homosexuals we have no wives and children. We can be brave without worry. We are the only ones to die." Frankly I hadn't thought of myself as a homosexual. I was a man who likes sex with other men. I also didn't think of myself as a spy, and I didn't want to be a martyr for France and Liberty. What he said was true, however. I was a homosexual and a spy and, unless I was very lucky, I might well become a martyr.

"I think I would rather live for France than die for her," I said. "But I am glad to know that I have been sucking the cock of a true French Patriot."

"It gives the Champagne of Man Seed!" Albert said, laughing. We returned to his bedroom and enjoyed the rest of the night.

Two weeks later Albert arrived in an official car with two companions and a chauffeur. Emile, the chauffeur, looked like a wrestler or boxer. He acted the role of a servile chauffeur unconvincingly. Louis De le Porte was an effete looking art historian and curator from the Louvre. The final member of the quartet was Jean Nouvelle, another curator. I soon found out he was Jan Noveki who had been at the National Museum in Warsaw. He had been an officer in the Polish Army who had escaped to France.

They stayed at my house and we went on a hiking trip into the mountains. It was difficult hike; our Neanderthal ancestors must have felt that difficult access protected them. Curiously De la Porte had no problem unlike his stronger looking companions. He climbed over the rocks as if he was a native of the area.

I led them behind a rock out cropping and then into a narrow crevice, at the rear of the crevice was a fissure, just wide enough to let a man slip through. Two meters into the crack, the space expanded into a chamber. Before us was the brilliant painting of the Blue Bear a superb work of art. I shone my light on it and Alan, Louis and Jan gasped in amazement.

"You presented this in Dresden and it didn't get publicized?" Alan said. "It's extraordinary."

"I found it the summer after my Dresden trip," I replied. "No one, except for me, knows about it."

"It's a wonder," Louis said. I took them down a dark tunnel like place and then turned to the side and went down another constricted space.

"Am I crazy, or is it getting warmer?" Emil asked.

"That is another surprise of this place," I said as we turned a corner. We could hear the sound of running water. We were now in a large cavern. It was broad and high and had several springs running through the room and a thermal pool. There was the faint smell of sulphur. There were cave paintings here, but only of the imprints of hands. There was no other figural work.

"This is great! Emile said. "While the traitors take the baths at Vichy, we have found our own spa. It's beautiful here." Emile had been quiet and seemed out of place in the group, but he was enthusiastic about the cave.

"We can say the place is decorated in Neanderthal Nouveau!" Louis suggested. Everyone laughed.

"There is one more room," I said. The water disappeared onto a crack in the floor. To one side there was another small opening. We passed through it into a domed space with a pool of hot water occupying three quarters of the room. There was no way for the heat to easily escape so it was hot, rather than warm.

"Is the water safe?" Louis asked.

"Perfectly. I had it tested. It isn't drinkable because of the high mineral content, but it is the same water you see in a spa," I said. "The water in the cool springs in the outer chamber is potable. There is some supply of fresh air here, because it doesn't smell, but I don't know where that is."

We had two oil lamps, so the lighting was dim. On the other side of the room there was a hulking figure, covered in hair and bear like.

I started, and then realized it was Emile. He had stripped naked and was looking for a place to get in the water. He found a place a stepped carefully into the pool.

"Come on in and join me!" he yelled. "The water is great!"

Louis and Jan were in the water momentarily. I was more cautious. I was no longer sure if my swimming skills after the automobile accident of several years earlier. My fears were groundless, the water was hot, but not uncomfortably so and salty, so you had a tendency to float on the top. In the dim light I couldn't see the men floating in the water.

My impressions of the men changed during the trip. Albert was every inch a Parisian and uncomfortable anywhere else. Jan was uneasy in the cave. I realized he must have suffered from claustrophobia. Caves frightened him.

Emile looked like a cave man and was entirely at home. Most surprising was Louis. He liked to affect the mannerisms of an effete pretty boy, but was physically strong and agile and seemed at home in the rough conditions of the cave. Emile and Louis could not have been more different physically, but they were both at home in the Blue Bear Cave.

CHAPTER 7

- In the Cave -

After exploring the cave we returned to my house for dinner. My Aunt had made a masterpiece of provincial French cooking, remarkably good given the food shortages. She was complimented generously. She beamed with pleasure and then told us she would need to leave for the rest of the week. A dear friend was sick and needed nursing care.

Emile volunteered to drive her to the home. It was five miles away and there were no conveyances other than foot. He would drop his party off at the hotel and then take her to the isolated farm. "It will be a bit crowded in the car, but we can manage."

"Perhaps I could spend the night and get to the Museum with Jean in the morning." Louis suggested. "That would alleviate the overcrowding." I said that arrangement was fine with me, so the men took off in the car with my Aunt.

Louis was excited about the cave. "Many people could hide there." he said. "It would be good in the summer, but in the winter wouldn't the tracks would be visible in the snow?"

"Footprints don't last in the mountains." I said. "The west side of that area is subject to strong winds. I went there last January and after fifteen minutes any trace of my footprints had been blown away." Louis looked relieved.

"I wanted to speak with you alone." Louis said. "I have some non political friends I would like to get to safety. Albert is very political. I am not. My friends are in danger, some are homosexual, some are Jewish, and some are homosexual Jews. I had many friends in the theater and art crowd in Berlin. I don't think that anyone here realized the full extent of the danger. The Nazis are beasts."

"I would love to help you, but winning the war is the main objective." I said. "I couldn't endanger the bigger objectives to save individuals." Louis looked at me.

"I understand completely." he said. "My plan is simple. I will use my friends as couriers whenever possible. Albert's thinking is to have Resistance members be the couriers. If they were to be captured, it would be a disaster. My friends are not important people. I would keep them in ignorance of the Resistance and thus they couldn't betray us."

"I guess that makes sense." I agreed, somewhat unwillingly. "It is very dangerous and physically demanding. Do you have friends who can do it?"

"That may be a problem, but I must be strong. I can only select those who can make it." Louis said. "However, let's face it. A Jew or Fag trying to escape from Nazi control is the most natural thing in the world. The border guards know that. No Jew needs to explain himself." We discussed his plan in great detail for the next hour. Louis had planned it very carefully. He was both detailed and imaginative in his approach. We talked late into the night in my darkened house. Electricity was turned off after 11:00.

There was a knocking at the door at midnight. I immediately thought that my luck had run out and the firing squad was waiting. I answered the door. It was Emile. He had dropped off my Aunt and had returned to get Louis.

"I'm glad you came." Louis said. "I have explained our little plan to Jean and he will help us." Emile gave me a bear hug.

"When I saw the cave I knew it was perfect. I misjudged you, I must apologize." Emile said. "I thought you were one of Albert's friends, willing but physically weak. I should have known you were all right when I saw you climbing over the mountain." We talked and I realized that Emile was the co-author of the plan. He had been a strongman in a carnival and bouncer at some not very respectable establishments in Paris. As a homosexual muscleman he had many admirers.

He was driven by a violent loathing of the Nazis and passion for his many lovers. He also thought he was a dead man anyway should the Nazis find him and wanted to save as many of his friends as he could. He had struck me as being sullen and taciturn when I first met him. He was friendly and open now.

We heard rain and wind. There was a downpour. I invited the men to spend the night. They agreed. I took the only candle and led them up stairs to the bedrooms. The house was cool since the spring hadn't been very warm and the house wasn't heated.

I showed them the guest bedroom and the bathroom and then went to my room. I undressed and put my robe on, went to the toilet and washed. Emile entered the bath. He stood behind me, undid my robe and felt for my cock.

"Louis and I were planning to enjoy ourselves tonight." he whispered, "Would you care to join us?" He paused and felt my cock. "Damn you've got a big one!" I was tempted.

"It's really late and I am very tired."

"Don't worry about that." he whispered. "Lou and I will do all the work. I haven't sucked one as big as yours in years. You can sleep and cum. You don't even need to be awake." I thought about telling him I wasn't interested, but his stroking had already made it clear that my cock was interested. Before I had a chance to answer he picked me up and carried me into the guest room. I am not a small man, but it was effortless for him.

A few seconds later I was naked in the bed with both men. Emile and Louis were good friends and they shared my cock. They bickered good naturedly as to who would suck for how long. They had totally different techniques. Louis deep throated me and used my cock to scratch his tonsils. Emile was almost delicate in the way he tongued my head. I was close several times with each. Finally I popped and Emile drank it down. I fell asleep.

I woke just after dawn sandwiched between the two men. The house had been dark and they had been at my cock so I hadn't seen the men naked. I didn't have much sense of what their bodies were like. I was shocked to see how badly I had misjudged them. Dressed, Emile was a dumpy, overweight man, naked he looked like more massive version of the muscle man Sandow, except for his dark complexion and coat of black hair.

Louis looked like an effete popinjay. Naked, he had a greyhound like slimness, all toned muscles without a suggestion of fat. He was a natural blond with a mat of darker hair on his chest and a stream of hair connecting his chest to his pubic hair. I moved and Emile got up to let me off of the bed. His cock seemed to be all head and balls. He was cut and the purple head looked as if it was the size of a ripe plum. The piss slit all but bisected the head.

I looked at it, dropped to my knees and took the head into my mouth. Even soft I had to open wide. I licked the tip with my tongue then flicked it on the slit. I could taste old precum on it. As I did, the slit parted and I found my tongue deep inside the head in the sperm tunnel. I got incredibly excited as my tongue worked its way deep into Emile's cock. I had never done that before, no one had been thick or wide enough to permit my tongue deep into the shaft.

Emile moaned oozed fresh precum as I explored deeper. Erect his cock was short, but remarkably thick. I found myself trying to force my tongue still deeper into the shaft. Emile liked that too. The tender lining of the tunnel responded to my tongue and we were both getting really excited. He tensed up and I knew he was ready to shoot. I rammed my tongue as deep as I could.

Emile bellowed as he climaxed and I trapped the cum in his cock. I could feel the sperm shooting against the tip of my tongue. I finally pulled back and he immediately filled my mouth with the product of his multiple ejaculations.

This woke up Louis who watched with amusement. I stood up with my mouth filled with cum trying to decide if I should swallow it or spit it out when Louis kissed me. Emile joined in and we shared his sperm.

"I love breakfast in bed." Louis said after we broke apart. "I've always liked kosher food." I understood Emile's hatred of the Nazis.

A month later I had the first guests at the Blue Bear Cave. Emile drove them to the museum. My building had been certified as a depository for works of art. We assumed that Paris would be bombed and my museum in a mountainous area near Switzerland was a safe place. The truck was labeled "Le Musee de L'Homme". It was filled with crates and boxes.

German soldiers watched every move at first, but Albert had cleverly filled the truck with Stone Age artifacts. The soldiers opened a few boxes and realized there was no gold or obviously valuable things. I had mentioned to Wolfie I was getting the shipment. I not sure, but I think he guessed there would be some Jewish cargo. He assigned his most slovenly and lazy men. I provided wine for their lunch. They slept the entire afternoon. The men from the Musee all dressed in the same uniforms and it was difficult to tell them apart.

That night I lead them over the dark trails to the cave. Much to my surprise there were six men. I had thought there were only three. One of the men had trouble, the mountain was more than he had anticipated, but he made it. He did not complain. Louis had selected his men well.

CHAPTER 8

- France, New Years, 1942 -

I learned in November that my parents were killed in the bombing of London. They had been watching for bombers on the roof of their hotel, when it suffered a direct hit. I had thought they were safe in England, but realized there was no safety anywhere in Europe. Samuel sent me a letter and said they were buried in his family's grave yard. DeGaul himself had attended the funeral. "All was done properly." he wrote.

My Aunt took it well. "An honorable death in these times is all you can hope for." she said. The next time I saw Wolfie he told me he was sorry to hear of my parents' death. I didn't know how he had found out, but the Free French radio had covered the funeral.

I went to the chateau for an official New Year's event. It was a dreary affair with the Mayor and Bishop and local dignitaries exchanging greetings with the General. Everything was very proper but I knew the Prefect of Police was a member of the Resistance as was the Treasurer of the Commune.

After translating for the official reception, General Wildebrandt took me aside. He was with one of his boys, Hans. Hans looked greatly like Siegfried, a hero straight from a Wagnerian opera. The General had told me Hans was hung like a horse, but didn't have the intelligence or the dumbest farm animal.

"My dear Jean!" the General cried. "I have a chance for you to help save the Culture of the Reich!" I must have looked appalled. He realized his mistake. "I mean to save some works of art. They are German, but they are art. Can you admire art without a Nazi taint?" I nodded. He got closer. "We have lost. The American's are in. The Russian's are in. It is over for us."

"You still seem to be adding victory to victory." I said.

"You remember I was a diplomat," he said. "I said the British would never surrender. Have you been to America? It is vast, untouched by war, and all but untouchable. Nothing but factories, raw materials and food. We don't have a single bomber that could touch her. If Churchill had asked for a divine favor of the highest order, he could not have asked for more than Pearl Harbor."

"Wolfie tells me you know all the caves in this area. Are there any suitable for storing works of art?" the General asked. "I have friends in artistic circles in Germany who want to save our art. Not the Nazi shit. I mean the Durers, the Holbeins, the real art. We figure it would be safe here. Unless Switzerland declares war on us, this is the most out of the way place in Europe." I agreed that this was out of the way, but didn't know how to do it.

"My dear Jean, you have perhaps noted that some of our leaders are noted for their rapaciousness. They seem to acquire art from the captured nations. I might be able to help you in some way." the General said.

"And how is that?"

"They don't take it from their fellow officers. I can confiscate the works, but turn it over to your museum. Your museum is a joke among the "Collectors." They have no interest in Stone Age tools. I will save what I can if you can help me save my treasures," he explained. He began to whisper. "I have access to a truckload of modern works, stolen from Jews in Paris. It is safer here than in Berlin." I said I would do what I could.

"Come to my private rooms for a drink, will you?" he asked. "These receptions make me dry." I followed them to the upper floor. His personal guard had cleared the house of guests and of the Gestapo agents who had been with us earlier. His rooms were sumptuously decorated and warm. There was little heat anywhere in France and the rooms were toasty. There was champagne on ice and food piled on a table. At first there was only the three of us.

A few minutes later Wolfie joined us with Max and Otto, my old professor. Otto looked tired and was much thinner than he had been before the war. We embraced warmly. He told me he no longer taught. He couldn't toe the Nazi line so he was now the registrar of collections for one of the museums in Dresden. To my surprise the General had been one of his students in Berlin. The General retained the very German awe of learned men and deferred to Otto as a great man.

Otto was afraid for the safety of the art work in his collection and had contacted Wildebrandt to see if he could find a safe place. The General felt that Dresden should be safe, but wouldn't contradict his former professor. Thus the General contacted me. I felt a lot better about the entire arrangement knowing Otto was at the root of it. We had several drinks and we all began to feel a bit more festive. Otto went off to the toilet and the General followed.

I didn't expect them back soon. I knew the Generals approach to sex and could guess what was going on. Wolfie vanished next. I realize my first coupling with the General and Wolfie hadn't been as spontaneous as I had thought! I smiled to myself. Otto looked as if he could use some cheering up and fucking a former student who was now a General in the Army might be just what he needed.

Max and Hans obviously were playmates and Hans was hoping the party would end early so they could go at it. Max winked at me. Hans didn't know I was a member of the club. I could hear Otto in the bedroom so I knew he was enjoying the General's hospitality. Max stood behind Hans and cupped his basket in his hand. Hans blushed.

"Hans, there's no need to be embarrassed. We're all men here," Max said. "You're a big boy. M. Le Director would be impressed! I'm sure he would admire your big German cock. Whip it out and dazzle him!"

"The general might come back!" Hans said. "He wouldn't like it."

"There is a private place around the corner. Go there," Max commanded. Hans did what he was told and we went behind a tapestry. It wasn't really a room. It was a big bay window which had been cut off from the room by the over sized tapestry. The alcove was big enough for a bench and little else. We were crowded. Max told Hans to get naked and the Nordic god striped in record time. Max was almost as fast and it took a while for me. My bad leg hurt my speed.

There were windows in the room, but the dim light from the moon provided only pale illumination. It was also cool. I felt Max's cock and remembered the good times in Wolfie's country home. Max directed my hand to Hans' crotch and the General had correctly described the soldier's equipment. Max directed Hans' hand to my cock at the same time.

"The General makes Hans fuck him every morning," Max whispered. "Hans is a good soldier and does what he is told, but he has an itch deep in his ass that needs to be scratched."

"I need it scratched so badly, Maxchen!" whined Hans. "You are the only one who has been able to reach it."

"Stroke the director's cock, Hans. Get it hard, so we can both get to that special spot," Max continued. "His is bigger than mine. It will feel wonderful." Max got me to sit on the bench and Hans bent over to suck me. Max oiled his cock and slipped it into Hans' ass. Hans was a big, imposing man with limited intelligence and I expected a quick blow job.

Instead, Hans was almost delicate in the way he licked and caressed my genitals with his tongue. I thought of him as a wine taster savoring a particularly good vintage. I thought of Emile and his approach and wondered if this had something to do with being muscle men.

Every time Max's cock hit the special place in Hans' ass, the man shivered and twitched. He was whimpering and I was afraid Max was hurting him. Then I realized the sexual feeling in Hans' ass were almost too intense for him. Max motioned to me to take his place at the soldiers ass.

I was going to oil my cock, but Max told me not to worry. "I shot a big load in there. He's wet enough," he said. Max was right. I was dripping precum and that, combined with Max's sperm, was just right. It was cold, but Hans was warm and his ass was hot. I slipped in to the hilt. Hans gasped.

"He loved it, Do it again!" Max said. I did. I soon found the same spot Max had toyed with. My cock is longer and much thicker than Max's. Hans was a size queen. He shivered violently when the cock head pressed the prostate. He was crying. I pulled all the way out.

"Please! Shove it in again! I can't stand it, but I love it!" Hans said. Hans and I were mismatched. My cock fucked him to distraction. His ass was nice, but didn't really excite me. It felt good and was enjoyable, but I didn't feel driven to have a climax. It was enjoyable enough to keep me hard, but not so enjoyable to induce an ejaculation. For Hans, this was a dream come true.

It was a dream come true for Max too. He later told me he really liked Hans, but he shot off so fast, Hans would jerk off before there was time for a second round and the sex was over. With me there, Max could fuck and shoot, then turn Hans over to me. I would fuck him for twenty or thirty minutes, until Max was ready to go again. Max would re enter his lover's ass and get a second chance to pop.

On this night Max got a good ten or twelve minutes of screwing in Hans' ass on the second fuck before he shot off. Much to my surprise, I wanted another round, and I had a slow and beautiful fuck. Hans was worn out by then and was almost asleep. He still twitched when my head rubbed him the right way. There was no resistance in his ass as my cock glided in and out on the sea of Max's cum.

There was a slight noise on the other side of the tapestry.

"The General must be in bed," someone said. "He might as well sleep. He will be on his way to Berlin in a week. We can then start the round up, without obstruction."

"The Labor Ministry will be pleased," the other voice said. "Quite frankly, I don't approve of the policy. Good German labor will do more in a day than conscripted labor will do in a week." I recognized the voice. It was a minor Gestapo functionary and his flunky. There was some noise on the other side of the room. "The microphone is working again," the flunky said. They quietly left the room. I suddenly recognized the other voice. It was Jules Davoud, he was the radio operator at the Gendarmerie and a collaborator.

I felt a shiver come over me. I was frightened. The Nazis were planning deportations. I also was climaxing. I couldn't believe that. At least now I knew, you could fuck a Germans soldier while collecting secret intelligence and have an orgasm without making a sound. I wondered if Mata Hari even came close to doing that! There was work to do.

CHAPTER 9

- The Round Up -

I told Wolfie the Gestapo's plans before I left the Chateau. He would inform the General. Wolfie told me that the General's first instincts were always to save himself. He would be worried about being sent to the Russian front. He would have no interest in saving French men from deportation to Germany. Wolfie said he would do what he could, but the Gestapo probable knew more about him than was healthy and any help would be limited.

I went home. It was three in the morning and my Aunt was awake.

"I was afraid they had arrested you." She said.

"Why would they do that?" I asked.

"I know all about the Jews and the people from Paris. If I could figure it out, they can!" she said. She was mad. Fortunately she was mad I had not confided in her, no one despised the Nazi's or their Vichy lap dogs than she. I told her what I had discovered about the deportations. I was trying to figure out how to get the word out. She burst out laughing.

"Dear Jean," she said. "You know that I am a virtuous woman, upright in every way. I do have one vice. Your mother, may she rest in eternal peace, scolded me about it for years. I am a gossip. I talk to other gossips and we make life difficult for some people who deserve it and some who do not I am afraid. I will get the word out. Everyone in the town will know by noon, unless they don't associate with women. I will leave that up to you."

"You know about that too?" I asked.

"It runs in the family, Dear Jean. It runs in the family." My Aunt had never married and suddenly I understood. I went to bed feeling good.

The next day was filled with activity. We had a new shipment from the Museum of Bronze Age pots and homosexual set designers from the Left Bank. I saw the Prefect of Police on the street and informed him of the problem in the radio department of the Gendarmerie. I spoke in very guarded terms, but he understood. He had already got wind of the deportations. My Aunt was as efficient as always.

Otto came by the museum and wanted to go looking for a cave in which to store his paintings. He had an assistant with him, Willie. Max was driving the car. I took them to the Elk cave that was in the opposite direction out of town from the Blue Bear Cave. The Elk Cave was just as secluded as the other, but was high on the side of a cliff, cool and dry. Otto was very satisfied. We returned to town and went to Otto's hotel suite.

I wanted to get back to the museum, but I promised to come by after diner to have a drink and reminisce. When I got back, the German soldiers had been called back to the Chateau. The General was expecting an important visitor, and there had to be an honor guard. This was a stroke of luck for us.

Emile was there but he was worried. The set designers didn't inspire confidence in their ability to climb over a mountain. I felt the same way, but Louis had good judgment, and I assumed they would make it.

I went home and found a note from my Aunt saying she had gone to the Convent of the Sacre Coeur and would be back the in the morning. My Aunt was a pillar of Calvinist rectitude, and I was puzzled. Then I remembered the nuns were teachers in the village's schools. They could warn their students.

I returned to the hotel and had dinner with Otto and Willie. Otto was gracious but uneasy. Willie was a classic German flunky. He idolized Otto and did his bidding, but never criticized or analyzed. Willie specialized in fawning admiration. Otto needed help. He was tormented by nightmare visions of Germany destroyed and Dresden burning. He was desperate to save any thing he could that could testify to the scholarly and cultured Germany that he loved and the Nazi's ruined.

At this point of the war it was hard to credit his fears. The Nazis were triumphant on all fronts. I tried to reassure him, to no avail. Wolfie appeared after dinner. We went to Otto's suite and had a drink. Otto was in the Bridal suite. A Nazi official was in the Royal suite. The Bridal suite was furnished in pink and white and Otto looked incongruous in the ultra feminine interior. I thought that conversation with Otto and me was Wolfie's objective for the visit. It took me only a few minutes to realize Willie was the prize.

Max whispered to me that he had given Willie a trial run the day before and thought the young man had potential. "He's inexperienced, but liked anything I tried." I hadn't looked at Willie again. I am not attracted to servile men and hadn't considered him as a sexual partner.

Willy was perhaps 25, average in height, and weight with a slight tendency to be pudgy. He looked soft. He had dark brown hair and a small mustache. I odd about Wolfie still hunting for men in the middle of a war, then I remembered the night before with Max, Hans and me behind the tapestry. I was fucking for France. I smiled at the thought.

"You look happy Jean," Otto said. "It is good to see you again. I feel much better."

"Even in wartime old friends are still friends," I said. He put his arms around me and gave me a bear hug. I had been careful about drinking, but no one else was. Soon we were in the bedroom. Otto and I were sucking each other. He had lost a lot of weight and this made his cock seem larger. I was curiously exited. I didn't know you could feel nostalgia sucking cock.

It was wonderful to be sucking his cock tasting his cock dribble, for a moment I was back fifteen years tasting his cock for the first time. I felt the same excitement. Wolfie and Willie entered to room.

"May we join you on the bed?" Wolfie asked. Otto climaxed. He ejaculated a rich creamy load into my mouth. He looked much older and almost worn out. I ate every drop.

"Please do." Otto said. "Willie is a nice boy."

"Is it all right, Herr Professor?" Willie asked.

"Of course, Wolfie and Jean are dear friends. We have always been very open," Otto said. "There is no combination of cock, ass or mouth when haven't explored freely." I was still sucking the seed from Otto's cock so I could confirm that.

Willie was more than willing to join in. Willingness and enthusiasm were his strong suit. He and Otto had a teacher-student fantasy in which Otto gave him sex lessons and Willie complied. Willie was a pure bottom, a sex toy. He just wanted to give pleasure. He wasn't muscular at all except in his throat and ass.

I wasn't sure I wanted to play with Willie, but changed my mind. Wolfie fucked him as Otto gave instructions. Otto told Wolfie where to poke and how to turn on Willie. I was holding Willie in my arms while Wolfie poked, then Otto got him to pull out and so he could demonstrate good fucking technique, Willie loved Otto's cock in his ass. Actually Willie liked it all. Wolfie traded places with Otto again and returned to plowing Willie's ass.

Much to my surprise, Wolfie shot off after only a few minutes. Otto re entered the willing man's ass as soon as Wolfie finished shooting. Otto pulled out shortly and was dripping. At first I thought it was Wolfie's cum, but Otto's cock twitched and a bead of cum emerged from Otto's slit and fell to the floor. It remained connected to the cock by a filament of cum. His cock twitch a second time and the blob stayed on the head. Both men had unloaded. I got into fucking position.

The second my cock head penetrated Willie's sphincter I knew why Wolfie popped. Willie's ass was a wonder, hot juicy and willing. He was really tight even with all the man cream lubricating his ass. Willie undulated his ass and rectum so his tunnel massaged my cock. Both Otto and Wolfie were good sized men, but my big meat gave him a jolt when I went deep. A welcome jolt, it seemed.

Willie had remarkable control over the muscles in his ass. At first I felt as if I were being milked, then he seemed to caress my cock with his rectum. It was a new and very enjoyable feeling. I understood when

Wolfie and Otto popped so quickly. Willie changed to the doggy style position so he could lick the sperm from Wolfie and Otto's cock while I fucked. This took some of the pressure off my cock, and I spent a long while in his ass. By the time I shot off, Wolfie was ready to go again.

We had several hours of this mindless fun. I returned to my cold house and slept as soundly as I had in months. My Aunt was back at seven and she was enraged. The master of Notre Dame College had refused to send any of his older students into hiding or to Switzerland. Father DeMoulin firmly believed that the Nazis and Vichy were the proper antidotes to communist and that the traitor Petain had France's best interests at heart. The College was a school for boys and many of the students were orphans. The Master even said he hoped some of the boys would join the Germans to fight the Russians.

My Aunt had been trying to convince the nuns to intervene on the boys' behalf. She believed that strong willed women could change the mind of Father DeMoulin. "The Mother Superior is an absolute fool!" my aunt ranted. "An idiot! She said that the good Father knew what was best for his boys!"

My Aunt was a staunch Calvinist and I had wondered if she would have any influence on the nuns. She was very forceful and must have thought that her own decisiveness would carry the day. She was wrong. She was still ranting when Emile returned from the cave.

"They are all safe." he said. "The mountains were filled with men alone or in small groups heading towards Switzerland. We spent half of the trip hiding from them. We thought they were Germans."

"They looked as if they were weak." I said.

"It was rough for them, but I didn't hear a world of complaint. One said he'd rather freeze to death here than did in a concentration camp."

Emile replied. My Aunt then went over her struggles with the Master of the Notre Dame College.

"If they go to Germany they will never return, you know?" Emile said.

"Of course I know that!" snapped my Aunt. "It's a death sentence. I don't know what to do!" This was an unusual confession for my Aunt. She always knew what to do. I went off to the museum, and soon was totally immersed in my work. I was filling my museum up with art from Paris museums, while I prepared a space to store German art work, while helping people escape to Switzerland.

Agreeing to store Otto's paintings was a brilliant move on my part. The General and Wolfie let me move freely and without surveillance. Even the Gestapo was pulled off. The General let the local Gestapo leader "discover" I was working for him and high ranking officials of the Reich. The fool got the impression I was smuggling valuable objects into the vaults of Switzerland to serve as safety net should the officials need to flee.

The General also launched a campaign to get his own troops into better shape. Drills and training sessions as well as parades and reviews became an almost daily feature of his troop's lives. Every soldier drilling wasn't watching the border. The German love of order was such, that no one guessed the General's true objective.

A week later, the General was called back to Berlin and two days later, a contingent of SS Troopers arrived. By then a good portion of the men of town had vanished. Old men and cripples such as myself remained as well as the non believers. Some men felt that their support for the traitors at Vichy would protect them against deportation. It didn't and I found myself hoping that they would suffer the consequences of their foolish fantasies.

The troopers tried to find out who was missing, but the records at the Gendarmerie were in a horrible state. The man in charge of them, who had also been the radio officer, had died in a freak fire. He had put gasoline instead of kerosene into a space heater and had been blown up. All the records were either burned or water soaked in the disaster. I had new respect for the Prefect of Police. Ruthlessness is a virtue in wartime.

The older students of the Sacre Coeur College were paraded into town by Father DeMoulin to volunteer for work in Germany. The good father had coerced them of course. My aunt was in daily communication with several of the Nuns who were their teachers. There was a bus in front of the Hotel de Ville, and about a dozen troopers. Most of the troopers had been sent off to the next town since there had been so few suitable males here. The head of the Gestapo was to welcome them to the service of the Reich in their anti-communist crusade.

There was a considerable crowd gathered. Most were dumbfounded by the treachery or ignorance of Father DeMoulin. Most of the boys were between 16 and 18 and were orphans or the sons of patriots who had disappeared, or been lost in the Fall of France. The crowd was sullen. I was watching with helpless horror from the window of my office facing the square.

Father DeMoulin was well known for his pedantic nature and the length of his sermons. He gave a speech that went on for a half hour. By that time the crowd grew considerably and I could feel the tension in the air. DeMoulin finished and the Gestapo officer rose to speak. As he did a strong, but very out of tune voice in the crowned began to sing the Marseillaise. I took me a second, but I realized it was my Aunt.

The troopers immediately raced to find the voice. Several others in the crowd joined in.

"Escape my Boys! Run to safety!" Someone screamed. From my vantage point I could see it was one of the nuns. There was pandemonium. Rocks and vegetables were thrown. The crowd surged forward and obstructed the troopers trying to find my Aunt. The boys in the center of the square vanished into the crowd.

I rushed downstairs to get my Aunt, but encountered six boys trying to escape. I took them to a secret compartment. Emile was there having delivered several Jewish intellectuals the day before. He took them under his wing and spirited them off to safety. I heard gunshots. Wolfie appeared with a platoon of heavily armed men.

He rounded up the troopers and the Gestapo agent and was giving them a dressing down that only an aristocratic Prussian officer could do.

"You are idiots! Fools! A disgrace to Germany and the Third Reich! You parade into the middle of town and you cause a riot! Then you let them all escape! I will report your gross malfeasance to the highest authorities!" screamed Wolfie. He was beating them with his riding crop, ranting, insulting and incidentally letting the boys escape. He must have gone on for ten minutes. I hadn't guessed Wolfie was a good actor. He was completely believable as an officer enraged at the conduct of his troops.

I could hear him screaming in the back ground as I searched for my Aunt. The square was a mess with rocks and debris everywhere. Most had left. There was no sign of my Aunt. I assumed she had escaped. A nun peaked out from a shuttered butcher's shop.

"She's here!" she whispered. Inside, my aunt was lying on the floor in a pool of blood, with massive bleeding from her head. She had been struck by a rifle butt. "I think his skull is crushed," the butcher, M. DeJardin, said. "If only M. Dreyfus was here, there would be a chance."

My Aunt's eyes opened. "That German officer told me they all got away." she whispered. "Is it true?"

"Yes. They all escaped." I said. She smiled, closed her eyes and died.

Mme DeJardin raced down the stairs from their apartment above with towels and bandages. It was too late. We all stood in silence as the nun, Sister Hélène, said prayers.

"A true hero," the butcher's daughter said. "She was like Jean d'Arc".

"Thank God that Boche Officer was so stupid. If he hadn't stopped the troopers, they'd have rounded them up again," the butcher said. "It was a miracle." A Gendarme appeared with a doctor. A minute later the Prefect arrived. He took one look at her.

"She died instantly?" he asked.

"No, she lived until I told her they boys had escaped." I said.

"That is why she is smiling?" the prefect asked? I looked at her. Mme DeJardin had washed her face. There was a look of almost serene satisfaction on it and a hint of a smile.

"Yes, M. Le Prefect."

"A brave woman," he said. "We can have no public funeral, no mention in the papers. The Germans are so embarrassed they would rather not let word of this event get out. If we keep everything quiet, there is a chance the boys will make it to Switzerland. That is agreeable?" I agreed.

"She deserves a hero's funeral!" Mme DeJardin objected.

"It is more important to save the living than to bury the dead," I said. We buried her in an unmarked grave in the yard beside the Protestant church the next night. It was only me, the DeJardins, two nuns, the Pastor and the grave diggers in attendance.

"She was a saint," a nun remarked.

"She was Protestant," I said.

"God selects the saints," the nun replied. After the funeral I went to the mountains to find Emile and the boys.

I got to the Blue Bear Cave and there was no sign of human activity there. Emile was a master of disguise. He told me that the set designers and given him some good ideas about camouflage. I slipped into the cave and got to the inner compartment and still hadn't found anyone. I decided to look in the pool.

Emile and two boys were soaking in the hot water.

"Jean, it's good to see you? What happened in town?"Emile asked. I told him.

"She was brave. She died well. What more can you ask for in these times?" he said.

"Where are the rest of the boys?" I asked.

"In Switzerland," he said, "it was a very easy passage. The Swiss are a lot better about Gentiles than they are about Jews. We picked up four more as we left town, so we saved a total of 12. 14 if you count the boys I kept for myself. Meet Georges and Jules."

They stood and shook hands. They were the oldest of the boys at the school and were full grown men as far as I could see. They had been too young to be drafted in 1939. That was three years earlier, so they had to be 19 or so. They were also were naked and half erect. This didn't bother either of them. George was thin, dark and tall with a long cock and the beginnings of a hairy chest. Jules was shorter, heavier but muscular with a down of hair thickening at his chest. Muscles were beginning to dominate the baby fat. His cock and balls were compact and held tight to his body. He would have a wrestler's body when he was fully grown.

Jules was Alsatian and spoke fluent French and German. George may well have come from the South, perhaps Provence. They seemed pleasant and very happy. I stripped and joined them in the pool. They both seemed to admire my cock.

"They boys and I discovered a common interest. The good Father was sending them off to Germany because they were orphans. He had molested them and wanted them to become priests. When they refused he turned on them. When we got all of the boys over the border, they wanted to come back to me. The Father liked to humiliate them by telling all of the other students what they were fagots. I agreed to bring them back," Emile said. "We discovered we shared the same interests and have been exploring them."

"That is fine, but this isn't a hotel. We'll need to find a permanent place for them," I said. George was playing with my cock. Something about the way he did it made me think that their experimentation had been extensive and successful.

"You are wrong. This is a hotel. We have people here all the time. It would be good to have someone here keeping it nice and prepared," Emile said. Jules is familiar with this sort of area, and Georges worked for his parents in a small hotel in Nice. They are hard working and sensible boys." I was afraid Emile was infatuated with the young men. That might have been true but he was a good judge of character too. The boys became invaluable as they maintained the cave. They were more mountain goat then men.

The school had been prison like and they had been abused for their sexual preferences. Emile and the cave represented liberation for them. All their sexual activity had been with each 'other and they weren't experienced. Emile was nothing if not experienced and liked to teach. They were willing students. As far as I could tell, they took to man sex as a duck to water.

They weren't at all like Willie, Otto's flunky. They were sex partners, not sex toys. An hour after we met, I was sucking Jules and Georges worked his cock into my ass. I would have complained, if it hadn't felt so good.

CHAPTER 10

- 1943 -

Jules and Georges were a real find. They were energetic, imaginative and strong. Within a week they had scouted out the entire area and were taking Resistance members across the border on their own. They also had an inexhaustible appetite for sex. Emile gave them a few pointers and they were able to figure out the rest.

We got along well. Emile and I had saved them, not only from the work camps of the Nazi's, but from the clutches of Father DeMoulin. Their discovery of the world of man to man sex was a revelation to them. They had played with themselves but were unaware other men shared their tastes for sex. I think if they had been in Paris or another big city, they would have been wild and they could have gotten in trouble. In the Blue Bear Cave they had only Emil and me. They also got to play with whoever was sent from Paris. Louis had good taste in men.

I was busy with my balancing act. I was getting shipments of artifacts from the Paris museums one week, then a container for artworks from Otto the next. The General had returned from Berlin he was much quieter and I knew that the situation there was bad. Of course by the summer of 1943 life was bad everywhere. Food and all of the necessities of live were limited. We were a somewhat rural district with many farms, but it was still difficult to live.

In June, Emile arrived on foot. Albert had been betrayed and captured. Louis had gone into hiding and the entire Resistance group at the Museum was broken up. Albert was executed without betraying any others, but everyone in the group was paralyzed with fear. Emile fled Paris and took up residence in the cave full time now. It was August before Louis was able to contact me again and reestablish the escape route.

We knew that North Africa had fallen and the Americans were looking toward Italy, but the situation in France only got worse. We were an unimportant area from the German's perspective, but that didn't mean they didn't bother us. The local Gestapo operative was a pathetic, low level bureaucrat, who wanted to rise to the top of that cesspool. He discovered my Aunt's heroic action and decided to punish her family. My house was confiscated and became housing for soldiers.

Wolfie tried to stop them. He suggested that beating the woman to death was typically considered to be adequate punishment, but sarcasm didn't work with the Gestapo. I moved to a small room in a poor section of town called the Bas Ville. I maintained my position at the museum. Even the martinet at the Gestapo knew I was doing favors for someone high up in the Reich.

This worked out well for me in a strange way. The Bas Ville was an old and poor part of the town. The residents had no sympathy for the Nazis or Vichy. With both my parents and aunt dead, they guessed I was involved in the Resistance, so they purported to have no idea where I lived, or where I was. I could come and go as I pleased. The Germans were uncomfortable sending spies into that part of the town. Any stranger stood out, so I was safer there than I had been at my house.

In late June, two visitors arrived at the museum from Paris accompanied by Louis. He had been able to reestablish the conduit from Paris and these were the first of a new group of escapees. Leo was a big, stocky, almost fat, middle-aged man. He was the editor of an underground newspaper who had been betrayed.

The other visitor, Raoul, was a former military officer in the French Colonial Army. He was distinguished looking, but appeared to be too old for active service. He wanted to join DeGaul. Louis returned to Paris. I was to take the men to the Blue Bear Cave. It was a dark and rainy day and we were able to slip away during a thunderstorm. The electric service was getting erratic as spare parts for repairs disappeared. A lightening strike could disrupt the whole town and we left in the confusion caused by a black out.

Much to my relief, both men had no problem with the arduous trek to the cave. We were all soaked to the bone when we got there and the dry cave never was more welcoming. I looked out at our path from the mouth of the cave. Our foot prints disappeared in the gravely soil before my eyes in the violent downpour.

We went deep into the cave and soon were in the room with the thermal pool. Emile greeted us. The boys were not there. We all stripped and hung our clothes up to dry. We got in the pool and warmed up. Leo was 55, bald, with a hairy body and big balls and a small cock. Naked, he was stocky, not fat. Raoul was tall and had been muscular when he was younger. He had a long cock and low hangers. He was modest and was a bit uncomfortable being naked in the cave. We had just got in the warm water when Jules and Georges returned. They had been hunting and had also scrounged up some vegetables.

Emile said he would convert the boys' finds into a soup and told them to join us in the pool. They stripped naked without embarrassment. The boys had been in the cave for six months and had matured considerably. Georges had lost his baby fat and was looking more muscular. I will swear his cock had grown so too. I mentioned this growth to Emile later. He said that was what exercise can do. Jules seemed taller and had become a young man. I caught Raoul glancing at Georges. He looked entranced. A second later he blinked and became a very proper French Officer. I knew he would like the boys.

Georges sat next to me and Raoul. He gave a complete account of the border guard patrols in the area and all their schedules. Jules filled in the geographical information. There were three trails they could take to the border, depending on the weather the next day. Raoul was impressed. The boys gave a thorough and complete description of the area and had plans, as well as back up plans, for every eventuality.

They had some plans for the night too. I wasn't sure the boys would be interested in the older men. Looking back, I admit I didn't think of myself as an older man. By this time I was a bald, bearded, hairy and lame man. I might not be everyone's idea of a dream boat, but I didn't think of myself as an older man. The boys got along with Leo and Raoul well. I suspected there was some reconnaissance going on under the surface of the water. The boys sat near the visitors. Emile returned. He had dinner stewing, so he stripped and joined us in the water.

"It will be a good hour or two before dinner is ready," he said. "We can have a nice soak. The boys have explained the plan for tomorrow?"

"Yes," Leo said. "Very thoroughly too. I hope you don't mind me saying I was uneasy with their youth, but I am totally satisfied now. I can relax." Emile laughed.

"The boys are totally satisfactory in many ways," Emile said. He put his arm around Jules and fondled the boy's cock under the water. "They are good at everything they do."

"It is war time," Georges said. "You learn fast, or you die."

"They take their work seriously, but they take their pleasure seriously too," Emile added. "I tried to give them lessons in pleasure, but I couldn't. They knew it all!" I was sure Georges had felt out Raoul and Jules was playing with Leo's meat under the water.

"Forgive their impetuousness," Emile continued. "They just escaped from a monastery type school and seem to be very curious about men."

"Are they your boys?" Raoul asked. I realized Raoul must have had some experience with younger men who were kept by older gentlemen.

"Not at all, we are all comrades here," Emile said with a smile. "They do what they wish." George got closer to Raoul and was obviously playing with the older man's cock. Soon he shifted so he straddled Raoul and then sat down. They were face to face and from their expressions I knew Raoul's cock was deep in Georges' ass. You could watch Georges glow as the feelings intensified.

I had an odd feeling it was more than sex. The two men connected. It was clear the first meeting of the men's cock and prostate was a success. It was hard to understand, but Raoul's cock must have connected to Georges' brain. They were one. Raoul was nervous and on edge until he skewered Georges. Georges obviously loved it. Oddly, I also felt Georges was in control. He was being fucked, but had Raoul in his power.

Leo and Emile were now sitting on a rock and Jules was sucking them. I joined them. Emile and Leo were similar physical types. Both men were stocky and hairy. Emile was much more muscular. The cocks were entirely different, however. Emile had a short cock with a huge head and the wide slit giving access to the inside of his cum shaft. Leo was average length hard, but very thick. The head was the same width with no flared edge.

I got engrossed in Emile's cock. I still was fascinated by having my tongue deep in his penis. Jules and Leo had hit it off well too. I stood to catch my breath and Leo saw my cock.

Soon we all were on a blanket on the floor forming a daisy chain, linked mouth to cock. Changing positions several times, we explored every possible combination of mouth and cock. Leo was a gifted cock sucker. His mouth and tongue barely touched the tender organ. Leo drank a sperm appetizer before dinner. I took Jules' full load.

The soup was good too. Emile had the French way with food. Whatever the raw materials he could find, he could convert it into something edible and indeed enjoyable. Leo and Raoul savored the dinner. Food in Paris was both sparse and aged by this point in the war. Old cheese and wine are one thing, Leo said, old lettuce was quite another.

As I left to return to my room in town, Raoul was on his back with Georges' cock rhythmically pounding his ass. The distinguished, older officer looked totally relaxed. He was motionless with a smile on his face and a slow oozing of precum from his cock. The dim candlelight caught the slippery fluid as a bead emerged each time the cock hit Raoul's prostate.

On the other side of the room, Jules lay between Leo and Emile. Jules was sucking Emile as Leo slowly and tenderly massaged Jules ass with his thick meat. I knew that Jules had his tongue deep in Emile's penis.

The trip home was uneventful. There was a steady drizzle and this made the tail difficult, but it kept the German troops indoors. The General had not inspired his troops to any display of devotion. They were fair weather troops only. That was fine with me.

At two in the morning, Max woke me. He said Wolfie needed to talk. I rushed to the Chateau through the darkened streets of the town. The place was pitch black, there wasn't a single light visible. Max took me into a stable, then into a tunnel to the main house. We were soon in a wine cellar. It was cool and dark. Max vanished.

A second later Wolfie entered, greeted me and introduced another man as Count Philip Von Eisenburg. The General was there.

"Count Philip is an old friend of mine," the General said. "He is more a brother than a friend."

"Actually I am a cousin," the man said in perfect French. "The general is more a brother to me than a lover." The general smiled. "I admit we have been friends, brothers and lovers at different times in our lives."

"Philip is a great lover," Wolfie said. "I can vouch for him in that regard."

"And what is the reason for these testimonials?" I asked.

"The Count is a patriotic German who is hoping to find a way to save the Nation from sure destruction. He and some friends are trying to find a way to... transform the leadership of Germany," the General said. I was going to say there was only one way to do that. I looked at Philip and realized he was fully aware of the only option.

"We are trying to open some channels with the Free French and the British," the General explained. "We need for them to know this is a serious group. We need assurances, should our group achieve their goals, the Allies will respond to a democratic government in Berlin. We need some independent verification of the Count's credibility."

"I don't know how I could help," I said.

"Jean, we know all about your activities in the Resistance and the Blue Bear cave," Wolfie said. "If any word of this conversation got out, we would all be garroted. We know and you know," I was shocked he knew. "I assured Philip you were safe; believe me when I tell you I am safe. You can trust me." He was right. We were all dead men if any of this was discovered.

"We need to get a message to Herr Westburg in Geneva," the General said. "No names, just something to let him know he will be receiving a message. We understand Herr Westburg trusts you." Philip then explained his plot in great and convincing detail.

"I will do what I can," I said, agreeing to be their intermediary. They all relaxed.

"With that done, let us adjourn to my private bomb shelter for a night cap," the General said. He pressed a button and a cabinet rotated giving access to another room. We entered and found ourselves in a luxuriously furnished space. It was warm and dimly illuminated. The General pressed another button and the secret door closed.

"A drink?" Wolfie asked. I nodded, he rang a bell. Two hooded naked men appeared carrying trays of drinks and hors d'oeuvres. It took me a second to recognize them, but the men were Max and Hans. They were wearing only hoods and rawhide straps bound around their genitals.

"Wolfie! You remembered!" Philip said. "You always were the prefect host." Wolfie smiled. A few seconds later the General appeared nude. "You both remembered!" Philip began to remove his clothes and Max whispered to me to follow suit. I did as I was told. I took a quick swig of my drink and it relaxed me a lot more than it should have. I was tired and the warmth of the room combined with the drink had a quick effect.

The General was in a lighthearted, almost festive mood. The Count was handsome. In his uniform he was much like Wolfie, the perfect Prussian Officer. He had a crew cut and close cropped mustache. Nude he was muscular and well defined, but was covered in a thick blond pelt, hairy front and back. In some light he looked smooth, in other he was a bear. His cock was cut, with a big head. The shaft seemed to taper as it touched his body. The constriction produced a natural cock ring. We talked and drank for awhile.

It was like a normal reception except we were all naked and the General and Count had no hesitation touching and stroking any cock in range. With the cock straps Max was half hard, Hans three quarters. I wasn't hard but had firmed up and my cock looked impressive in its slightly excited state. When they bent over I saw they both had butt plugs sealing their asses. I remembered Hans' interest in ass play and I could tell he was enjoying it.

Max handed me another drink. The General asked Hans for one of his special drinks. Philip smiled. He told Hans to bend over. With the mannerisms of a magician, he tugged on the butt plug and withdrew it. It was a large dildo. Philip unscrewed the base and poured a drink from it. Philip then reinserted the dildo-flask. Wolfie and the General applauded.

"I found it in the United States during prohibition," he said proudly. "I won't say I discovered it in the most elegant place in America, but it was, perhaps the most exiting bar I found there." He gave the glass to Hans who hung his cock in it. Hans pissed in it, added ice and gave it to the General.

I was shocked, but titillated too. These were new aspects of homosexual life. I had thought water sports were associated with humiliation and degradation. I had no interest in water sports at all, but it seemed to be the General's interest and was harmless. The General was drinking the brew with obvious enjoyment. I remembered him sucking my cock as I pissed. It was his choice.

I was thinking about the odd scene before me when Wolfie started to suck my cock. I was hard and I felt relief that real sex was under way.

CHAPTER 11

- *Winter 1944* -

I had joked with Samuel about being an unusual choice to be a "Mata Hari" type spy. Nothing Mata Hari could have done could have been more bizarre than the events of the next two hours. I was the only Frenchman in the group, but I will admit I, or more correctly, my cock, represented the Third Republic well. I had never participated in a sex marathon before, but the General, the Count, Hans and Max all wanted my cock.

All got it. At first I had the image of a French museum director being assaulted by the jack-booted officers of the Third Reich. In reality, I did the assaulting, starting with the Count and ending with Max. The Count was a vocal bottom, who moaned and cried the entire time I was in his ass. I was uncomfortable fucking him at first. He had a tight ass and my cock didn't fit well. I tried to pull back when he winced in pain, but the General wouldn't let me.

"He loves it, Jean," the General said. He was right, even though my cock seemed to hurt the aristocrat. The Count maintained a huge erection. There must have been a connection between the pain and sexual arousal in his mind. By the time my cock was fully lodged in his ass, his erection was magnificent. I don't think I rammed him more than a dozen times before he began to shoot.

The General was next in line. He started with a huge erection. My cock slid into his ass effortlessly and he glowed in pleasure. He must have been working on his stamina. I screwed him for a good ten minutes, and then Hans took my place. I had a good erection, but wasn't particularly excited by the men, so it was the ideal situation for a long session. The General's ass was enjoyable, but I felt no urge to shoot. Curiously, Hans seemed to feel the same way. He spent another ten minutes in the General. We traded places. I went five or six minutes before turning it over to Hans for a second session.

I knew Hans was a bottom and wanted my cock in his ass. When the General began to look a bit frayed after the heavy fucking, I popped into Hans' ass. Hans slowed his fucking of the General as I pumped him. I knew how much Hans liked that. He slowed as my cock began to take control of his ass and he soon emptied his load in the General. Hans and the General both moaned in satisfaction. I was sweaty and hot after this and went to the adjoining bath. There I found Wolfie and Max in the shower.

Max bent over and Wolfie removed the flask from his ass. Wolfie offered me a drink and I took a swig, then he popped a glass ampoule for me to sniff, took a snort himself and passed it to Max. It was incredibly potent amyl nitrate. A second later I slid my cock into Max's open hole.

I had the sensation of being safe at home in my own bed. My cock was home in a friendly ass. A few seconds later, I felt Wolfie's cock at my hole and I opened up to let him in. The three of us turned into a single fucking mass. Every movement Wolfie made was directly transmitted through my cock into Max's quivering ass. After a few minutes of coupling, we broke apart to catch our breaths.

The minute Wolfie freed his cock from my ass we knew it was too good to stop so we traded places; I fucked Wolfie as Max screwed me. It was just as good. Max's cock must have grown since the last time we played. It made a direct hit on every sexual nerve in my body. We finally cooled down. Wolfie popped another ampoule and I rammed him as he did Max. I began to shake as the pressure for the orgasm began to build.

The Count suddenly appeared, pulled me off Wolfie and sucked my cock. My dick already had been in five men's holes, but that didn't bother the Count at all. I began to ejaculate and not a single drop escaped the Count's greedy mouth. He was like a man in the desert dying of thirst who just found an oasis.

The General arrived and sucked Wolfie's cock as he pulled it from Max's ass. I saw Wolfie was still shooting as the General's mouth enveloped the dripping dick. Neither man seemed to mind the mingling of cock and ass.

We rested for a short while, but I became aroused again. Not just aroused, I was horny as hell. I think there must have been something in the drinks. Everyone had shot off, but erections were rising. Count Philip was next to me. Our eyes met and we kissed. My ass began to twitch and I was overwhelmed with a desire to get a cock into it. The Count must have sensed this, as he stroked his cock to full erection.

He got on his back on the floor and I straddled him, and then sat back. He had a big mushroom head which barely fit through my sphincter. The shaft was thick, but tapered at the base. It became more comfortable, the deeper it went. My sphincter clamped tight on the shaft and his cock was trapped in my ass. Philip didn't fuck; he just lay there and moaned in pleasure.

I was undulating and twitching, massaging his cock and my prostate. His cock was in my ass, but I was in charge. It was good for me and for him. It only got better. I relaxed and looked around the room. Max was rough fucking the General and Wolfie was in Hans' ass. The General was crying in pleasure.

I twitched and Philip's cock twitched too and got even harder. It must have occupied another part of my ass and I lost all restraint. I was doing an exotic dance on his cock, wiggling, grinding and thrashing any way I could to get any more feeling from his cock. Philip's eyes glazed and I could feel his cock shooting deep into my ass. I began to shoot, spraying across the room. My sperm landed on Wolfie's back. Wolfie had finished with Hans, so he came over to suck my spewing cock. He sucked me dry, and then kissed Philip, sharing my juices. Hans came over and licked my spunk off Wolfie's back. He kissed me and I tasted my own cum on his tongue.

I got home at five in the morning and got a few hours sleep. When I got to the museum Emile had another shipment of antiquities arrived from Paris. This shipment was complete with three downed British fighter pilots. It would be a full day.

Thinking back, I realize sex is only sex and no more, but I did feel trust for the Count. I knew Wolfie and the General were all right. I knew they were risking their lives. Several weeks later, I went into Switzerland and went to see Samuel. This was a legal border crossing as I was translating for the Mayor in negotiations with a German-speaking government official in Bern. This was a weak excuse, since most Swiss officials are multi-lingual, but our Gestapo commander had limited understanding of the world.

The Mayor never questioned my activities. He was a cautious man and never committed to either side directly. In his heart, he may have been pro-Vichy, but Vichy was only a memory now. They weren't even pretending to be anything but puppets. The Mayor was fully committed to the welfare of the town and while he wouldn't directly help the Resistance, he was always helpful when it came to protecting the community.

Samuel met me at a museum in Bern. He looked ten years older and I was a bit shocked. He looked shocked too. I saw myself in a mirror and realized we had both aged. I was getting gray and quite thin. I told him of the plot. He thanked me for the information, but had no other reaction.

I told Samuel about the art storage. He already knew about it. This information was transmitted to the Allies and we were out of bounds for bombing.

He gave me all the other news of the war. North Africa and most of Italy were in Allied hands and the war was going badly for the Germans in Russia. France would be liberated next, but no one knew when or how. There were plans for internal uprisings in France, to pull German troops away from the main Allied invasion. We remained the safest escape route from Paris, so no insurrections were planned for our district. Samuel said the end was in sight.

The tide had turned, the end was inevitable, but the destruction continued without abatement. I had spent years in Germany and knew most to be good people, but they had let the devil have control and they couldn't get power back again. It seemed that they and Germany were doomed. They would pull down most of Europe with them.

Years before I had spent a week at Bayreuth listening to Wagner's Ring. Wagner always struck me as an odd combination of genius and crank. The ring combined sublime music with perverse sex. It worried me that it appealed to Hitler. Gotterdammerung, the Twilight of the Gods, in which the gods destroy their entire world rather than return the ring to its rightful owner, seemed to foretell the ultimate result of the Nazi lust for power.

Everyone knew the final result of the war, but no one knew who would survive it. Some ignored this. Our local Gestapo office became more oppressive. The manpower shortages in Germany made the dragnets for men more thorough. Our local Gestapo toad still dreamed of transfer to Berlin. He didn't know there might not be a Berlin by the time the war was over.

Our situation deteriorated when General Wildebrandt was transferred to the Embassy in Lisbon. His replacement was a martinet, General Obermayer. He had been wounded badly on the Russian Front. He was a true believer in Hitler. In nearly constant pain, he seemed to know something wasn't right under Wolfie's command. He hated Wolfie and all the members of the old aristocratic officer corp. There weren't enough arrests and executions. He set out to rectify that situation.

His hatred for Wolfie was greater than his detestation of the French. This worked to our advantage. Obermayer could not speak a word of French, indeed his German was none too good. I was called in all the time to translate. I was a fixture of sorts. My German is perfect and he seemed to forget I was French.

Wolfie wasn't a particularly brave man, but he returned Obermayer's hatred with a vengeance. Wolfie looked like the perfect Prussian officer and to him the General was lower class trash. He fought Obermayer at every opportunity. Wolfie was never direct, never straightforward. Minor delays and obstructions continually confounded the Generals plans.

The Mayor and the Prefect of Police shared Wolfie's opinion of the new commander. The Prefect was always sly and calculating. I got the impression the Mayor was getting some backbone as the situation deteriorated. He was naturally a verbose man and he began to afflict the General with lengthy meetings. The General had less time to work his evil plans.

The Prefect seemed to know all the informants and double dealers in the city. There were always Gendarmes near the museum and when one of these creatures appeared, they would let us know. We began to get couriers bringing information back into France. I assumed they were bringing instructions for the Resistance about the eventual invasion of France.

My cave containing German art was filling up. The clearance for these shipments came from very high in the German Government and this gave me some protection from both the General and the Gestapo. I could vanish and they assumed I was going to the cave. I let them know it was important I not be followed, since that might give the location away to the French residents. By this time even the Gestapo admitted their agents were known.

The Gestapo was afraid of the district I lived in, so I was left alone there. The streets and alleys were narrow and roof tiles often dislodged when a German passed by.

Samuel notified me Raoul was to return. I had thought the officer was too old to serve with DeGaul, but he was put in charge of Free French activity in our Province. I knew he had wanted a more active role in actual combat. I think Georges made the return more palatable. Raoul brought a younger man with him, a radio operator. For the first time, we would have regular communication with London and the Free French government.

I got to the cave late in the day to see Raoul.

"Jean, I brought a friend for you. His name is Robert," Raoul whispered to me.

"I have a lot of friends already," I said.

"Trust me," he said, "You will love Robert. He is a scholar, he was at Oxford when the war started and was unfit for service. Poor eyesight. He joined DeGaul as soon as he could. Robert is a patriot and scholar. He shares our sexual interests."

"I thought your interest was Georges," I asked. Raoul burst out laughing.

"Yes, I like Georges," he said. "You will like Robert!" We went into the cave. Emile was cooking; Georges and Jules were on watch. The only other man was a stranger. I assumed he was Robert. He looked tall and thin with a newly grown, brown beard. He introduced himself as Robert De Champ, said hello and addressed me as "M. Le Director" with great politeness. In the confusion of the war, I had almost forgotten my rank. In spite of the war, I still had impressive academic credentials.

He knew all about my work. He had been working with Neolithic Stone Age finds in England and Scotland. When I got close to him, I realized he was slightly below average height. He was proportioned like a tall man. After a half hour of conversation, we were friends. We shared the same interests, same approach to life and same likes.

He had a speech impediment, due to a cleft palette. It had been repaired well and he spoke well. The beard disguised the surgery. His parents were from Normandy. He hadn't heard from them since the fall of France. That seemed odd, since there was little fighting in Normandy during the fall. Then I remembered he told me his home was in Normandy. I recalled the Banque DeChamps of Caen and I put one and one together. The Banque DeChamps had an association with the Rothschild family and while the DeChamps were Protestant, that might not be enough to save them.

Georges and Jules returned with another man, Wing Leader Evans of the RAF. Evans had been one of the downed pilots shipped with the antiquities from Paris. He had been wounded in the crash and the villagers who saved him had not been able to set his arm correctly. He had escaped to Paris and then was sent by Louis to me. His arm was partially paralyzed, so his flying days were over. In Paris he heard a village had been burned and the residents shot or sent to concentration camps for helping downed pilots.

Evans realized it was the village that saved him. Given a choice between piloting a desk in London and fighting the Germans in France, he opted for France. He stayed. He wanted revenge. This concerned me. Revenge can cloud your thinking.

Evans seemed to be attracted to Emile. We never called him anything but Evans, but I had no doubt he was upper class. He had been to Oxford and had been an upper class gentleman before the War. Emile was near the bottom rung of French Society. They were a strange pair.

I suspected Emile and Evans planned to be more active in the liberation of France than DeGaul wanted. I was worried their plans might endanger civilians in the area. Emile told me not to worry. That didn't reassure me at all.

Robert had stared at Evans when he entered. I thought he recognized him, but the look vanished and Emile announced dinner. Emile was a master of creating a diner out of nothing. This was noodles and a mixture of vegetables and greens in butter. We were in a dairy area and butter was still available. It was simple, but tasty and filling.

It was Georges' turn for watch duty. I offered to do it, so he and Raoul could make up for lost time. Outside of the cave was cool, but pleasant. It was a clear, dark night with no moon, so the stars were spectacular. I realized this was the same view prehistoric man saw from the entrance to the cave. They too would have felt the awe of the star filled heavens. I assumed they had a watchman, although watching for a wild animal was preferable in my mind to watching for Nazis.

I heard a noise from inside the cave. Robert emerged.

"Is it all right if I join you?" he asked.

CHAPTER 12

- France Summer 1944 -

I hate to be thought of as being predictable, so I was slightly offended when Raoul told me he had selected Robert for me. He was sure I would like the young man. He was right. Robert and I saw the world in much the same way. We liked the same things and were just different enough to be interesting. He seemed to have a limitless ability to work and to learn. That first night, keeping watch under the stars, we became friends.

Ever since I met Wolfie, I had screwed first and become friends second. Friendship was an enhancement for the sex. With Robert, I had the opposite experience. We liked each other so much; the friendship was the dominant theme. I was actually a bit afraid the sex wouldn't meet the standards of the friendship. Robert was shy.

He was tall and thin, with a long thin cock. Robert had big, low hanging balls that looked over sized for his slim body. He had a hairy chest and body. He always looked manicured and his hairy body always looked as if he had combed it. At first I thought he wasn't too interested in man sex. That wasn't true at all, he was reserved and it took a while for him to get use to the free and easy attitude of the cave. That was not a problem, as it turned out.

I discovered later Robert had some bad experiences in England and was careful about making friends too quickly. He also seemed to have been brought up under the assumption that sex consisted of one partner using the other for his pleasure. Apparently the concept of mutual gratification wasn't part of his upbringing. He had guilt feelings when he enjoyed himself and was suspicious of men who wanted to have sex with him. His sexual experiences were limited and not very successful. Robert had no idea what he was missing.

I solved the problem for him. I was attracted to him, but hadn't guessed he was all but infatuated with me. I had been hoping he would let me suck him. He was dreaming about sex with me. When we finally got together, the moment my tongue touched his cock, he was drawn to mine. We were cock to tonsils in a second or two and neither of us wanted to stop. He copied my actions, licking the cock head, or deep throating the entire cock.

We shot off together, sucking up each others jiz. Robert was young and had a raging hard-on an hour later. I impaled myself on his cock. Later, I found out Robert hadn't thought fucking could be enjoyable to the bottom. He had tried it at Oxford and his partner didn't like it. He knew better by the time he shot off in my ass. I loved it.

I was the first man he fucked who enjoyed it. When he stopped worrying about his partner's feelings, he relaxed and let loose. It was intensely enjoyable and shy Robert screwed me three more times that night. It was as if his balls were over producing cum and he had to shoot it all in my ass. That was fine with me.

When he was hard, his cock bent down, rather than up. I discovered this the first time he screwed me doggy style. His cock rammed the base of my cock instead of going up the chute. It felt as if his cock was trying to get in mine. It was an incredible sensation.

Robert was shy, except where his balls were concerned. He was proud of them and the man cream they produced. They produced huge amounts of semen and he loved having them played with. He never initiated sex, but once he was aroused he was a great lover. Robert loved for me to roll his balls in my fingers and play with his cock. He leaked at the first touch.

Robert's cock felt great in my ass, but my meat was a size or two, too large for his ass. He was willing enough, but it simply didn't fit. We would work on that.

In some ways, Robert was much like Georges and Jules, but he was much more intellectually mature. He was able to plan and calculate; he could understand the consequences of our actions and anticipate problems. Our district of France was largely untouched by the worst of the war. I wanted to keep it that way.

Robert became my right hand man.

Back in town, General Obermayer was a problem. His bitterness and hatred of all things French were extreme. The disaster that was beginning to befall Germany just increased his rage. He was by nature a destroyer, a hater. He began to proclaim increasingly strict limits on the residents.

Our area was free of any organized anti-German activity as far as he knew, but he began confiscation of food and equipment. Automobiles disappeared, as did tractors and the town's buses.

When possible, Wolfie or Max slipped me advance warning of these moves. The farmers of France are a wily lot. They were never particularly pro government even for the Third Republic. Most calculated how much to let the Germans take and saved the rest. They had a sense of what was a seemly confiscation. There was enough, but not too much for the Germans. They disabled much of the equipment, so it was of no value. The hardships of the last few years made the lack of spare parts credible and they saved a good portion of their equipment. They also hid most of their livestock.

One night, Max appeared suddenly at my room. He was in civilian clothes and was scared to death. Wolfie had received a coded message from Berlin. The Count's plot was discovered. Wolfie had some incriminating records at the Chateau, so he had stayed behind to destroy them. He told Max to save himself.

Max didn't know if the entire plot was exposed, or if one or more of the plotters had been captured. We all knew of the Gestapo's interrogation techniques, so there was little hope the entire plot would not be known soon. All the plotters were in imminent danger. I told Max to stay in my room and I went to the Chateau to get Wolfie. I knew he would not be able to keep my secrets under torture.

I got there too late. The place was crawling with Gestapo agents and troops loyal to General Obermayer. There was a lot of confusion and yelling as the Gestapo tried to get in and Wolfie's men tried to delay them. There was a single gunshot. Why, I don't know, but I knew Wolfie committed suicide. We had been friends for years and I realized as a good Prussian aristocrat he couldn't face betraying his friends. He also couldn't face torture. He made the right choice to insure we were safe. I returned to my room.

"He's dead, isn't he?" Max stated. It was a rhetorical question. He knew too. "Did the Gestapo get him?"

"No," I said. "He shot himself."

"That is best," Max said. "He was a good man, too good for these times." I took Max to the cave. The Gestapo was patrolling the streets and it was difficult to avoid them, but we managed. The Mayor had been arrested as was the Prefect of Police. That didn't make any sense to me. Later we found out one of the plotters had talked and the Nazi's knew of the visit to this area. The Count had met the Mayor and local dignitaries and they were arresting anyone who had come into contact with. I guessed the Nazi's were trying to make the plot look as if it were French rather than home grown. I realized I couldn't return to the town.

No one was very happy having a German soldier in the cave, but they relented in their opposition when I told the story. That night, they discovered Max was a sex maniac. Wolfie received some early hints as to the discovery of the plot and Max had been in terror for weeks. He was too frightened to have sex. When he got to the safety of the cave all of his pent up sex drive exploded.

If you want to make friends fast with a bunch of homosexual men, get on your back, open your ass wide and tell everyone the bank is open for deposits. This was Max's approach and it worked like a charm. Even Emile found something to like about the diminutive German. Emile fucked Max hard, no holds barred. Max liked it that way and the rougher Emile got, the better Max liked it. When I woke the next morning, I saw Emile and Max sleeping together.

Max opened an eye and winked at me. He gave his hips a few thrusts. I knew Max's cock was massaging Emile's prostate and all was well with that pair. Emile tended to be selective about who he let in his ass. He had obviously lost his distaste for German cum.

Around noon a messenger came from town and told us they had executed the Mayor and had hung Wolfie's dead body from an electric pole in the town square. The Mayor had nothing to do with the plot and little to do with the Resistance itself. I realized that being safe and careful in war time wouldn't save you. I never thought much of the Mayor, but he died bravely.

Oddly, they let the Prefect of Police go free. He was involved with the Resistance up to his eyeballs. A few days later the Prefect had Wolfie's body cut down and buried in my family's plot, next to my Aunt. I hadn't realized the Prefect knew about my relationship with Wolfie. Clearly he did.

General Obermayer had no restraint on his activities now. He prepared to unleash a reign of terror on the district. The walls were covered in proclamations and new rules. Death by firing squad was to be the punishment for any and all crimes. This was hard on the town, but good for us. We were a conduit for information and people from London to the underground. Obermayer concentrated on the town and left the mountainous areas alone, with only perfunctory patrols.

I hadn't wanted any violence from our men, since the area had been so peaceful. It was no longer peaceful, so I let Raoul, Emile and Wing Leader Evans hatch their schemes. They decided killing Obermayer was the most direct approach to solving the problem. All plans went into high gear on June 6. It was late in the day when we found out the Allies invaded Normandy. While our area wasn't scheduled for an uprising to divert German troops away from the front, we knew it would be hard for the Nazi's to respond in force to a problem in our area.

I knew a lot about Obermayer's schedule, since I had been his translator. He lived in the chateau under heavy guard, but Max knew all the passages and cubbyholes of the place.

"If there is any place in the castle big enough for two men to get into and screw like rabbits, I've found it!" Max proclaimed. "I also know who would like to kill him among his own troops. He has many enemies. No tears will be shed when he dies."

"I think an accident would be ideal," I said. Emile brightened at that suggestion. "Our General might fall down the stairs, or out of a window."

"I used to arrange accidents all the time," he said. "It's not sporting in the way our Wing Leader likes it, but it does the trick, none the less."

"It was not sporting at Remy sur le Marne, was it?" That was the town that sheltered Evans after he was shot down. The villagers had been machined gunned. "He should die like the dog. No the rat he is," Evans said. "I would not do to a dog what I want to do to him."

"I would like to finish off Father DeMoulin," Georges said, "It would be a great example to traitors in the future."

"No revenge!" I said. "We are doing this for France." It was Georges turn to be on watch, so he left. I was stiff and decided to try the thermal baths. As was typical, everyone else seemed to have the same desire. Evans and Emile were friends as I was with Robert. Jules was the odd man out, but since Georges was on watch, Raoul was available for play. Max was available for anyone who wanted him, of course.

Jules was getting bigger and more muscular as he aged. You could tell he was going to be bald by the time he was 25, but his body hair was growing and thickening.

Robert asked, "Is it required that we have sex every night? I don't mind it, but I can't recall any place I've been that does it. It is a bit odd." I was fondling his balls below the water and I knew he wasn't objecting to sex.

"You know, I think sex is just about the only activity which can drive the thoughts of war from my head," I said. "If I fall asleep with a cock in my mouth after an orgasm, I sleep well. Otherwise, I dream of the war.

"Damn if you're not right," Evans said. He had been listening. "The war, my bad arm and more war were all I thought about until Emile rammed me with his cock. I never was fucked before," he continued, "Afterwards, I slept for the first time in two years."

"I fuck because I like it," Emile added. He smiled ruefully. "When I was younger, men paid to sleep with me. Many men are excited by a brutish looking wrestler. It paid well, a lot better than being a wrestler. I got so bored with it, I thought I had lost my taste for sex. The minute I walked into this cave, I loved man sex again. It was as if I was twenty and sex was still exciting."

"You mean it's not really exciting?" Evans asked. He had a skeptical look on his face. "I can't visualize you as being cool and detached while you are plowing an ass."

"Well, I wasn't as enthusiastic then as I am now," Emile said. "I haven't liked a cock as much as yours in years."

"And you have sampled a good number of cocks?" Jules asked. Emile laughed.

"Half of Paris! Give or take a few hundred," Emile confessed. "I know cocks! Take it from me; this cave is filed with the crème de la crème".

"You have tried them all?" Robert asked.

"All! Except yours," Emile said, with a tinge of sadness. "Mans' sexual anatomy is a puzzle. You can lust after a hot stud and find out he is little more than a damp washcloth in bed, yet you take a little troll for a ride out of pure pity and go to the moon, the sex is so good. You never know, unless you try."

"You don't need to try them all," Robert suggested.

"Why not?" Emile retorted. "I'm not looking to have your babies, or live with you for the rest of my life. I'm looking for a little fun, that's all. I don't ask for more. We are all adults, aren't we? I try what I want and if my partner is agreeable, why not?" Raoul was sitting on the other side of Robert and I encountered his hand exploring Robert's genitals. Robert laughed.

"I'm afraid you are right! We might as well help each other out," I said.

"Eat, drink and be merry for tomorrow we die," Emile added. "I like to think when the Nazi's get me, my cum will have filled my friends' asses and every time they think of me, they will feel a twinge in their ass! Maybe their cock will twitch a bit." Evans laughed.

"You are a romantic!" he said. "Remember, when you die, you'll take a few pounds of my seed with you. I didn't shoot in you to have it wasted by the Nazis."

"Enough talk about sperm. I'm hungry, who wants to server me some man seed desert?" Raoul asked. Georges and Max both volunteered. Max took Raoul in the ass while Georges fed the distinguished looking officer.

"I know Robert is yours, but I would love to taste his cock," Emile whispered.

"Robert can do want he wants," I said. "He makes so much cum, there is always some left for me. Sometimes his second load of the night is bigger than the first." Robert was listening and glowed. He was proud of his balls and the globs of sperm they produced. He was excited by the chance to demonstrate his sperm making prowess. Emile would be sure to appreciate it too. I had enjoyed sex with Emile and thought Robert would like it too. They paired off.

Evans and I were left over and made the best of it. The Group Captain was reserved until he got hard, then he was a wild man. In contrast to his reserved and somewhat effete manner, his love making was rough and ready. Emile had introduced him to the joys of anal sex several months before. Now he was a confirmed bottom and loved it doggy style and rough. Unfortunately heavy duty man ramming makes it hard for me to hold back and I shoot quickly.

I could hear Robert moaning as he shot off in Emile's mouth, as I rear loaded Evans. Evans collapsed on the floor. He had shot off too. Emile and Robert came over to me and we embraced. Emile kissed me and Robert. He had saved Robert's entire load in his mouth and as we French kissed the sperm drooled out of his mouth.

Robert's cock was semi erect after the climax. As soon as he tasted his own cum in Emile's mouth, he became rock hard. I knew exactly what he wanted, so I turned around and bent over. Emile dropped to his knees to suck Robert and lubricate his cock with spit. Seconds later, Robert's cock head was seven inches in my ass, pounding my prostate.

I don't know if he shot a bigger load in my ass, or in Emile's mouth moments before. Robert shuddered and shivered each time he shot a volley of cum in my ass. I counted twelve ejaculations when I had a second orgasm. That was like a lightning bolt out of nowhere. It was totally unexpected, but extraordinarily satisfying. Emile was still on his knees and intercepted the sperm as it shot from my cock.

We all kissed again, this time sharing my cum.

CHAPTER 13

- France Late 1944 -

The Nazis were finished, defeated and on the run. Cornered rats are the most dangerous. I knew our small town was entering the most dangerous phase of the war. Obermayer was a mad man. He second in command, Col. Weiderman, was a former manager of a Berlin Department Store. He had no taste for war at all.

Max was with us full time and gave us a rundown of the personalities of the German forces. Oddly, Max found his courage after Wolfie's death. He told me he was afraid of being tortured by the Gestapo, but as long as he could fight, he was with us.

For most of the soldiers, there was no desire to do anything but go home and protect their families, if that was possible. They still obeyed, but they had no desire to carry out the General's more draconian plans. Max also knew the members of the "Brotherhood of the Cock". Both Max and Wolfie were sexually generous and had many friends. Obermayer was violently anti-homosexual and had no problem punishing those he had the slightest suspicion of.

Most were demoted to menial jobs. The General tried to get them sent to the Russian Front, but the clerical part of his office was slow to the extreme and I'm not sure if anyone actually made it to the Russian front from our area. You know an army is defeated when the soldiers are trying to select which armed force they will surrender to. The universal hope was to be captured by the Americans or Canadians. The English were third and then the Free French. At the very bottom of the chart were the Russians.

Hans, my old playmate, was now working in the motor pool. The need to dispose of Obermayer was getting greater as he turned more vicious. Emile wanted an ambush. I wanted an accident. Shortly after the liberation of Paris a Resistance ambush killed three German's near the town. To this day I don't know who did it. It certainly wasn't anyone under my command.

Obermeyer took hostages and announced he would shoot them all in a week if the Resistance members weren't turned over to him. Our plans shifted into high gear. Obermeyer was paranoid and rarely venturing out of the Chateau now. A full frontal attack on the castle seemed impossible. We didn't know exactly where in the labyrinthine building he slept or worked.

Raoul, Emile and Evans worked on a scheme to attack the chateau as a decoy and stage a jail break to release the hostages. Good luck intervened. Max had friends in the enlisted men. Max had shaved and now was unrecognizable as his former self. But he was just as good a cock sucker as he ever had been. He hooked up with Hans and discovered Obermayer's Achilles' heel.

As part of his purge of homosexuals, Obermayer had discovered and become infatuated with a young kid, Eric Meyers. Eric was a very young looking 18 and the General was smitten. He had told the kid he could escape transfer to the Russian Front by becoming the General's boy. It was very hush hush since Obermayer was officially anti-homosexual, but the kid was brought to the General's bedroom several times a week to get screwed by the General. Eric had been a virgin and submitted, but hated it. Hans had proudly told Max, he had given the boy a lesson in man love. When Eric found out what real man sex was like from Hans, the boy grew to hate Obermayer more. The General needed his partner's pain to have an orgasm.

Eric knew exactly the General's location in the castle was. He knew his schedule and normal working habits. Max of course knew the castle well and pinpointed the places which were subject to attack. Once we knew the location of the General, the military men went to work fast. The General liked to fuck Eric just before the kid was on watch. Eric would get reamed, then spend the night on the tower in the cold with his ass filled with cum.

The General varied his days, but almost always screwed Eric on Saturday night. That was the last possible chance to get the hostages out since the executions were to take place Monday at dawn. Raoul and Evans led the attack on the castle. Emile and I led the attack on the prison. Eric was on the midnight watch and would signal us which room Obermayer was in that night. It was a cold, dark night in early fall, with no moon. It was a long wait before we could move into position. I was with Robert, Emile and Georges. We went to the museum. It wasn't guarded at night and we all knew all the hiding places in the building.

We got in place after nine and had nothing to do until we heard the attack on the castle. I was nervous as hell. I had been under constant threat of arrest for years and was accustomed to that. I had never done anything violent before. I was uneasy about shooting someone. The only shooting I had done was from my cock into a German mouth or ass. I was more like Mata Hari than I wanted to admit.

I told Robert and Emile how nervous I was. Robert said he felt the same way. Emile laughed.

"I guess it must be inexperience." I said.

"Not at all." Emile replied. "I've been in a lot of tough situations. It's easier to be attacked that to attack. When you are assaulted, every atom in your body resists and goes on the defensive instantaneously. When you are on the attack, you have the advantage of surprise, but there is always hesitation. Some might call it cowardice, but I think it's something more basic than that, the urge for self preservation. The basic human urge is to avoid violence."

"I wish there was some way to relax." Robert said. "I feel as if I'm going to blow up in so nervous."

"I've got an idea." Georges chimed in. "If I die, I want St. Peter to meet me with my balls empty and my ass filled with my comrades' seed." I laughed.

"That sounds like something Wotan might appreciate at the entrance to Valhalla." I said.

"If I go to Valhalla I'm pretty sure none of the Nazi scum will get in. They attack the weak." Robert said. "I do have a suspicion Wotan wouldn't mind his cock in a brave man's ass. He didn't seem to care much where he shoved his cock. I don't know about St. Peter."

I wasn't too sure about Emile's suggestion. Fortunately, my cock and balls had no question about the appropriateness of the "tension release scheme".

"You take care of Georges first." Robert whispered in my ear. "You've never fucked him. He thinks you still think of him as a boy." I looked at Robert. He knew I wanted his cock in my ass. "Don't worry, Jean. You know there is always more and I am always ready!" Robert smiled.

On the other side of the room Georges and Emile had stripped. I joined them. Emile gravitated to Robert. George and I got together. I was really eager to get together with Robert, but Georges turned out to be a much better experience than I had guessed.

He had been a kid when I met him when he escaped from the Nazi roundup for the labor camps. Now, there was no baby fat left as far as I could tell. He had matured and had a man's body. I had also not looked at his cock lately. He was usually with Raoul, so I had never experienced his meat. It was pure man meat, thick, heavy and juicy.

Raoul and Emile had taught him all he needed to know about homosexual sex. He was enthusiastic and skilled. I was hard five seconds after he started to suck me and on the edge of shooting a minute later. We slowed up and 69ed. He was a mouthful, but his cock fit my mouth perfectly. I was so preoccupied with my thoughts about Robert, lust for Georges snuck up on me.

Georges was dribbling precum and his cock juice went straight to my brain and then to my balls. He whispered to me, he had never been fucked by a cock as big as mine. Georges had been sucking and slobbering all over my cock, so I was lubricated. In a quick movement, he shifted and his legs were pinned on my shoulders. My cock was poking at his hole.

He resisted for two or three thrusts and then he opened wide. I could feel him react to the pain of the penetration, but the second my cock head passed through the sphincter, Georges was fine. He was like a wild horse, which only needed to be broken in. Usually when I fuck a guy for the first time, I am careful not to hurt him.

Georges would have nothing of that. As far as he was concerned, the harder and faster the better. I screwed him like a wild man. Needless to say, I didn't last long. I shot off and left my cock in his ass to drain all the man seed. I was relaxed when Robert came up behind me and stroked my ass with his dripping cock. I opened up and Robert slipped into my ass.

I was afraid he was mad at me for fucking Georges with such obvious enjoyment. In fact, it had excited him. He spent a quiet quarter of an hour massaging my prostate with his cock. I thought I wouldn't be able to respond after the terrific orgasm in George's ass, but male sex organs are resilient.

Robert's cock was long and thin, with a big mushroom head. He just slowly pumped my ass and soon enough my prostate began to respond. My cock got hard again and I fucked Georges a second time. Robert shot off in my ass and pulled out. Emile had been resting after his session with Robert earlier, so he came over and sucked on Georges until the boy came a second time. The contractions of his ass as he shot were enough to make me shoot a second time.

We went back to our waiting. I opened the window of the attic space we were hiding in to make it easier to hear the attack on the castle. That was lucky for us. I was looking out when I saw flashes in the direction of the attack. I didn't hear a sound. The wind or the atmosphere kept us from hearing anything.

We raced down to the street and ran two blocks to the Town Jail through dark, back alleys. As we arrived, a truck left the jail with most of the German guards. They were off to reinforce the castle. One German was guarding the door. He was busy watching his departing comrades and we got behind him and had a gun in his back before he knew what had happened.

We used him as a shield and got in the building. Inside there were only Gendarmes, most of whom I knew. I told them to disarm, and turn over the hostages or we would shoot the guard. The senior French officer looked at us in mock horror.

"Disarm men!" he said. "Do anything they ask. We must save our German friend!" The Prefect's men had been trained well. They remained helpful but always covered their ass. They could say they lost the hostages because they had to save the poor guard. I looked at the guard for the first time. It was Hans. He winked at me. We got out as fast as we could. We locked the German in a cell and the gendarmes in another. We got the hostages out of the building.

Outside the Gendarmes had already cut the phone lines to the building so they wouldn't be able to get a call out. Outside the town was still quiet. There were no more flashes, but we raced the hostages to the museum. One was badly beaten. We broke up the group into three parties. Leaving one group of two at the museum with me, another went directly to the Swiss border with Robert and the third went to the cave.

The beaten man was with me and I tried to help him. The other hostage was a young man named Steph. He was a farm boy and said he would go home. Once he got in the mountains they would never find him. He vanished in the night.

I cleaned up the man and recognized him as Jean Moulinier, a watchmaker. He had broken ribs from being kicked and was in great pain when he tried to move. He tried to help himself and me, but the pain was so great he couldn't stand it. I realized I was trapped at the Museum for a day or two until I could find a way to move him.

The town was still quiet and I had no idea if the attack on the castle had succeeded. The Gendarmes were in the streets at six, making great show of hunting for the hostages. I was in my attic hiding place.

The secret door opened and a police man entered. It was the Prefect of Police and the Police Surgeon. The Doctor brought painkillers and put Jean to sleep with a shot. I was shocked to realize the Prefect knew my hiding place and knew which hostage was with me. Steph was his nephew. The boy knew how badly hurt Jean was and had told his Aunt about the situation. Jean was one of the Prefect's agents in town and the Germans had been trying to beat him into betraying his comrades.

"You may relax, General Obermayer isn't dead, but he will be shortly." the Prefect said. "Only the best medical care could save him and he can't get that, even his own doctors aren't that foolish. The British are 20 kilometers away and will be here tomorrow. I must go and meet with Col. Wiederman in an hour. I think I will discuss an orderly transfer of control. No more fighting, no more deaths. He is a most sensible man."

I went back to the cave, leaving Jean in the doctor's care. From the hill above the town I could see activity at the Castle. Some trucks were leaving. I wondered if they were pulling out. I had a suspicion that many of the men in our remote location would prefer to be captured to fighting to the death. They were afraid of reprisals for the destruction done to London and Rotterdam earlier in the war.

It seemed there was an element of poetic justice to this, but I couldn't feel good about any destruction. So much had already been lost. Raoul and Jules were at the cave with Max. The attack had been successful but not easy. The General's personal guard put up a stiff fight, but a grenade had ended resistance. A grenade blast had left Obermayer without legs and an arm.

Raoul had brought two prisoners with them. They were locked up in the rear cave. I went to see them. It was Hans and another soldier I didn't know. Hans had been sent from the cell in the Police Station to the Chateau, just in time to be captured by Raoul.

"Max said they were good men, anti Nazi, but we needed someone else to vouch for them." Raoul said.

"I know Hans well enough. He may not be anti- Nazi, but I know he is no threat. The other man looked up. At first I didn't recognize him, and then I realized it was Fritz Dalham, the man I have met at the Professor's retirement party. He was in an enlisted man uniform.

"Fritz, how did you get here?" I asked.

"Deserting, trying to escape from being executed," he said. "It's not a pretty story." Fritz had been a wealthy man, and I knew that wealthy men did not become enlisted men in the German Army. He was dirty and looked weak. When I had seen him in Dresden, he had looked like a Greek God.

"It has all been a disaster." Fritz said. "I thought I was restoring German greatness and now we will be lucky if anything survives." Max and I untied them and we went to the thermal baths to clean them up.

The baths helped some. Fritz was despondent. Naked, some of Fritz's spectacular physique remained. Raoul was watching as the German stripped. His suspicion turned to interest as Fritz stood nude in the cave.

Hans was uneasy. He had been captured and released twice and wasn't taking anything for granted. He was in good physical condition and he got admiring looks from Emile, who had returned to the cave.

With Emile was Samuel Westburg. Now that the war was all but won, he had reverted to being Samuel Wertheimer, the name he used when I first met him at Wolfie's country house. He seemed over joyed to see me. He knew of Wolfie's death, but took it as a natural part of war. He didn't seem to be worried about Hans and Fritz.

He told me the thermal bath looked really good to him, so we joined the two Germans in the pool. Max joined us and it was almost a reunion.

CHAPTER 14

- Peace -

In the pool, we all relaxed, or at least tried to relax. It is hard to turn your emotions on and off, especially after the excitement of the day's events. It didn't seem possible the war was coming to an end. We were a collection of Frenchmen, Germans and a Jewish Englishman sitting naked in a thermal pool under a mountain. Emile, Fritz, Samuel and I were bilingual, so we were all able to talk and translate for the others.

Samuel told us about life outside our little part of France. I had thought there was nothing left of London after the Blitz. He told me there was lots of damage, but London was still London and so were Paris, Rome, Florence and Venice.

"Paris is the same?" Emile asked.

"Almost untouched," Samuel said. "It needs a good paint job, but it's the same."

"Brussels is in good shape, so is Amsterdam," Fritz said. "I was stationed there."I don't know if they will be able to rebuild Rotterdam. That didn't look possible." He paused. "I don't know if anything will survive in Germany. I was in Cologne and Frankfurt three months ago. It was hard to believe the destruction. I saw it with my own eyes and still can't believe it. I can't imagine what is left of Berlin or the cities to the east. They say Dresden had all but vanished." Fritz was on the edge of crying.

"The destruction isn't over yet. Buzz bombs are still falling on London," Samuel said. "I wandered through the city several months ago. It's cold and damp and there isn't much food, but St. Paul's is still there. It's like a surrealist painting. The Cathedral sits there serene and majestic in the middle of blocks of ruins. Nothing survived except the Cathedral in that part of the city. St. Paul's looks undamaged."

"England and France will at least survive the war. I don't know if Germany will," Emile said. "I don't know what the Russians are planning. The future may not include Germany."

"How could it have happened? Germany was the center of education and culture. Science and art, Mozart, Hayden, Beethoven, Wagner. Nothing but ashes now." Fritz was near tears again. Max and Eric appeared with Evans. They were excited from their attack on the Chateau. They saw us nude in the pool and I never saw men strip so fast.

They explained Obermayer was dead and the Garrison surrendered to the Prefect of Police. The city was liberated. Max recognized Fritz and looked suspiciously at him.

"I thought you were a Nazi agent?" he said. "You were at the party in Dresden."

"I was supposed to be an informer. I thought I was. I just couldn't do it," Fritz said. "I was supposed to watch you and report incriminating conversations to the Gestapo. I was shocked when Jean didn't get the award. His paper was brilliant. I still had faith in the master race, how I could have been so stupid, I don't know."

"Things were good when it was all flags and marching and victories against weak nations. We were so disciplined and obedient, it didn't seem anyone could stand against us," Fritz added.

"Least of all those weak, effete democracies. Who would think England would hold out? When America entered the war, we were doomed," Max interjected.

"When I met Wolfie in Berlin all this didn't seem to be possible. I was French, he was German and we had no problem at all," I said. "We all got along personally and professionally. Of course we were all united by a common love of cock."

"I'm not 100% sure, but I think we all still may be united by a love of cock," Max said, as he launched himself at Fritz's cock. Emile translated the comment into French. Everyone laughed. Everyone also seemed to be inspired by Max's example.

"Is this the time to suck and make up?" Raoul asked with a smile on his face. Hans looked at him. He couldn't understand French, but he seemed to get the drift. Much to my surprise Emile seemed to be taken by Fritz too. Soon everyone in the pool slipped into sexual play. There were no Frenchmen, Germans or Englishmen only cocks and assholes.

I remembered Fritz was a bottom. I hadn't realized he was an insatiable bottom. It was a good way to make friends. Hans was handsome enough and affable enough to be acceptable to everyone. Samuel, Max and I got together and relived old times. It was strange to have my cock sliding into an ass for the first time in more than a decade.

Robert returned from shepherding his men to the Swiss border. He walked in while I was deep in Samuel's ass. He didn't blink an eye as he joined in the festive orgy. Robert got behind me and worked his cock into my ass as I ploughed Samuel.

Robert was usually shy about fucking, but he wasn't shy at all this time. I was sandwiched between one of my oldest friends and one of my newest. I loved Robert, but the sex had never been that exciting. I liked Samuel, but the sex had always been good, very good.

Robert's cock popped through my sphincter and as it slipped deeper into my ass, it got better. When he was four or five inches in my ass, it became fantastic. By the time his pubic hair touched my ass, I was in heaven. My cock seemed to have directly transferred my excitement to Samuel and somehow I knew Robert was as excited as I was.

Strangely, we all seemed to plateau and then stop. I had that "few seconds before orgasm feeling" for a good three or four minutes. Every inch of my cock had bonded with Samuel's ass and every movement was exquisite. Robert's cock had become a part of my ass. The feelings were so spectacular I couldn't tell if it was my cock, or Robert's which was generating the feelings that all but overwhelmed me.

"I can't hold back anymore!" Robert cried. He pounded wildly, then became still. I felt the sperm shoot into my ass. The force was so great it almost tickled. A second later my balls exploded and I shot off. Samuel moaned as his cum spurted from his cock like a Roman candle. As I ejaculated, my ass twitched and Robert moaned. The triple orgasm wasn't just good, it was a good as it gets. We collapsed on each other exhausted. I didn't want to move. My cock felt good, trapped in Samuel's ass.

Robert was young and didn't lose his erection after his orgasm. He stopped thrusting, but if I moved, he would pump a few times to freshen up his erection. We finally broke apart. Robert and I went to bed together.

The next day we went back to town. The Prefect was in full control and greeted the advancing British troops. Our entire group was together. Every one of us was back from Switzerland and there had been no casualties from the last days' events. I thought our group was unknown, but the whole town treated us as Resistance heroes. Even stranger, they all thought I was the leader. I was apparently known as M. Le Neanderthal. Wing Leader Evans was with me on the side of the street.

"Evans! You're bloody alive!" a man screamed from a jeep. He jumped out and ran over. "You may not believe it, but I went to your memorial service!" After a few minutes, Evans introduced me to his old friend Archie MacDonald. Archie was almost a caricature of a bluff and hardy Scot with copper hair, a bushy beard and barrel chest. He was in army khakis, but he needed a kilt and a sword to be complete.

The day was confused. I was suddenly a member of the town council and I was also asked to go to Paris to meet with the Free French government. Robert had to go to see if he could find his parents, or any members of his family. He hitched a ride with a messenger and vanished.

A week later, MacDonald took Emile and me to Paris. I was to go to the Louvre and meet with some fellow curators and discuss the recovery of looted objects. I also wanted to tell them about my own treasure trove of art objects from German Museums. I was given rooms in the Hotel Georges V. Apparently my fame as a curator-Resistance member had spread as far as Paris. I couldn't figure out how this happened until I remembered Samuel. I was working for him and he alone knew what my group was doing.

I was given a double room, so both Emile and Archie stayed with me. At the Louvre the remains of its staff were trying to figure out where everything was located and if it was hidden, looted or just lost. The Musee de L'homme staff, which occupied another wing of the Louvre, was all but gone. They had run an underground printing press and had been betrayed. A representative from the Army wanted me to go with them into Germany to identify and protect art works as the nation fell into Allied hands.

I told the Acting Director of the Louvre about my stores of German art. He felt it was best to keep it quiet until the war was over. If the art was safe in my caves, it might as well stay there. That made sense to me. I didn't get to Germany until 1947. There was too much work to do with our own museums. Because I had German connections and had maintained good relations with several Germans, I was in a good position to help locate looted art in Germany.

I had many long days at the Louvre, as we worked out the problems and figured out approaches to finding stolen art. Samuel ran an office in Switzerland that watched art galleries and dealers who were trying to sell stolen paintings. Samuel seemed to know most of the crooks and con artists. I knew the names of German Curators and historians who could possibly help. My name was known in certain German circles as being able to protect artwork. Emile retained good connections in Paris' underworld. We had saved some of them from the Gestapo. He was a good source of leads as to stolen objects and likely fences. The three of us seemed to cover all the options.

Archie was on leave for two weeks and stayed with us. He was an attractive man and good company, but he created a sexual dry spell for Emile and me. The sex had been great in the cave, but having a third man who was hetro sexual in the room, put a damper on sex during our stay at the Georges V. We were all adult men and perhaps we could have ignored him, but it seemed rude to have sex with him in the room. That all changed when Emile and I walked in on him with a young Naval officer. Archie couldn't have been more embarrassed. Emile resolved the difficult situation by stripping naked and joining them.

I followed suit and the four of us had a good time. The Naval officer, Willem De Groote, was Dutch and found Emile very attractive. I liked Archie and seeing him naked and excited did nothing to reduce that. Archie was well hung, thick and massive. Archie was also a size queen and my cock all but mesmerized him.

It had been a long time since Archie had last had sex and he wanted to make up for the lack. He said he was a top, but he wanted my cock badly. I oiled his cock and he oiled mine. Much to my surprise, Archie opened his ass and opened it wide. I touched my cock head to his hole. Archie shivered in excitement.

"I've never taken a cock as big as yours before," Archie whispered. "I want it, but go slow and take it easy." I pushed forward and Archie's ass offered no resistance. My cock head popped in and my shaft began a slow progress deep into his body.

It turned out Archie not only liked to look at big cocks, once I was fully lodged in his ass, my cock was everything he hoped and expected. He loved it. There was nothing my cock could do he didn't enjoy. My horse cock penetrated into unexplored parts of his body, parts that were virgin. He was in ecstasy and his enthusiasm spread to me. It was a wild sexual romp.

Emile and De Groote got caught up in the play and joined in when they could find an opening. By the time we woke the next morning, we had explored every possibility and configuration of sexual coupling. It was a night of pure sex. None of us were lovers; we were just friends. Each of us was ready, willing and able and there was no baggage to keep us from exploring our bodies and those of our companions.

This was my last night of all-out sex for months. With the end of the war, the men I knew all dispersed to their homes. Robert was gone for three months and my communication with him was sporadic. Telephone and even mail service was erratic. There was a chance his parents were alive, but his Father had been carried off by the Gestapo and his Mother had simply vanished. Robert's sister and brother were in the United States, working as translators at the State Department. They had access to leads as to his parents' possible whereabouts. Robert was able to check out some of these, but to no avail.

When I got back home, there was so much work to do; I didn't miss the companionship of my friends for months. Nothing had been done in five years for maintenance and repairs in the town, so there were almost daily breakdowns. There was an outbreak of crime and no one knew what the franc was worth.

I met Robert only briefly after the war. He found his mother in an asylum in Spain. She had suffered a total mental break down. His father was liberated from a concentration camp in Germany. His health was broken, but he felt he had obligations to the family bank and their depositors. Robert was now helping them full time. Robert had always been a responsible man. That was one of the things I liked about him. I knew in his heart he had no option other than to return to his family obligations. There was no way we could resume our relationship.

Max stayed with me. He had no relatives in Germany, at least not any he wanted to stay in touch with. He became my valet-assistant. It was nice to have some contact with my life before the war. Max never said it out loud, but he wouldn't leave Wolfie. Wolfie was buried beside my Aunt.

In late 1946 Archie came to see me. I hadn't realized, but Archie was a wealthy man, the son of a Scottish nobleman and he had liked my little town. It was good to see him. He was good company and we had a nice visit. I showed him the other tunnels and the Stone Age paintings. He was impressed.

"This is such a beautiful place," Archie said. "The caves are a treasure. I would love to explore them more."

"Are you interested in stone age paintings?" I asked. "What are you interested in?"

"It's odd. My Grandfather was interested in Stone Age Culture. He did some excavations of early sites in Scotland. He published the work and was apparently much admired at the time. I thought it just boring stuff old guys liked. I've been thinking more about it now and it seems more attractive. Lately though, my primary interest has been modern men's cocks. I seem to be a bit obsessed with them." I laughed.

"That seems fair to me. I share the same interest," I said, "Have you been trying some out?"

"Ever since our roll in the hay at the Georges V, I've been sampling some. I'd played a little in school, you know, boy stuff. It didn't seem to be worth the effort then. Your cock was twice as big as anything I had tried before and at least four times more pleasurable."

"Well, I'm glad I pleased."

"You did a hell lot more than please, Jean," Archie said. "I've never felt anything as good, before or after." He paused. "I was hoping you had liked it too?"

"I did, but I'm not sure I liked it as much as you did."

"Well I was hoping we could try it a few more times and fix that problem," Archie said. "Would you be willing to give it a try?" I said sure, but I was promising nothing beyond some fun in bed.

We did have fun in bed and a lot more. It had been a wild romp at the hotel a year earlier. Archie had been fun and responsive. Somehow this time, Archie all but sucked my cock into his ass. It was one of those rare occasions, when your genitals merge along with your physical sensations. I felt as if my cock belonged to him and I needed his tender ass lining to make me complete.

Archie was a big, bluff, bear of a man, strong and commanding. It was always hard for me to believe such a strong man had an ass so delicate, tender and quivering in excitement. Archie stayed for a week and each night the sensations grew stronger, more exciting and more totally involving. He came back a month later and stayed for the next twenty years. We were happy.

ABOUT THE AUTHOR

- Bob Archman -

Bob Archman lives in rural Virginia in the shadow of the Blue Ridge and finds writing gay themed adventure fantasies and a pleasant way to spend time. He is interested in older, mature men many of whom aren't conventionally regarded as attractive. He discovered many years ago not even gay men can stay young forever. Most aren't flamboyant hairdressers, florists or interior decorators as is often portrayed in the media. Bob is interested in stories about everyday working guys who don't fit the stereotyped images of gay men.

Bob Archman is also the author of *Clydesdale & Company* and *Clydesdale Goes to the Hunt*. These books and more at Amazon.com, TheNazcaPlainsCorp.com or your local bookstore.

Clydesdale
& COMPANY

Archman

CLYDESDALE & COMPANY

A NOVEL BY
Bob Archman

A BONER BOOK

Clydesdale

GOES TO THE HUNT

A NOVEL BY

Bob Archman

Archman

CLYDESDALE GOES TO THE HUNT

www.ingramcontent.com/pod-product-compliance
Lightning Source LLC
Chambersburg PA
CBHW070823250626
47170CB00006B/2192